"Are You Telling Me to Leave?" She Asked.

"Well, one might say it's my turn," he said wryly. Reaching out, he cupped her chin in one hand and tipped her face up to meet his. In spite of her struggles, he did not release her but continued to hold her face and study it with brooding eyes.

After a moment, he suddenly took his hand away from her chin and, with a tender, relentless pressure, brought his strong, sensuous mouth down upon hers.

Her own traitorous lips softened under the demanding pressure of his, parting in welcoming surrender. . . . She knew she should tear herself free, but she had no will left to move.

LEE SAWYER
began her writing career as a journalist but switched to her true love—romantic fiction. Her work and travel experiences give her novels an authentic sense of setting, while her engaging and fluid prose carries the reader throughout her lively stories.

Dear Reader:

During the last year, many of you have written to Silhouette telling us what you like best about Silhouette Romances and, more recently, about Silhouette Special Editions. You've also told us what else you'd like to read from Silhouette. With your comments and suggestions in mind, we've developed SILHOUETTE DESIRE.

SILHOUETTE DESIREs will be on sale this June, and each month we'll bring you four new DESIREs written by some of your favorite authors—Stephanie James, Diana Palmer, Rita Clay, Suzanne Simms and many more.

SILHOUETTE DESIREs may not be for everyone, but they are for those readers who want a more sensual, provocative romance. The heroines are slightly older—women who are actively involved in their careers and the world around them. If you want to experience all the excitement, passion and joy of falling in love, then SILHOUETTE DESIRE is for you.

I'd appreciate any thoughts you'd like to share with us on new SILHOUETTE DESIRE, and I invite you to write to us at the address below:

Karen Solem
Editor-in-Chief
Silhouette Books
P.O. Box 769
New York, N.Y. 10019

LEE SAWYER
Time Remembered

Silhouette *Romance*

Published by Silhouette Books New York

America's Publisher of Contemporary Romance

SILHOUETTE BOOKS, a Simon & Schuster Division of
GULF & WESTERN CORPORATION
1230 Avenue of the Americas, New York, N.Y. 10020

ISBN: 0-671-57156-7

First Silhouette Books printing June, 1982

10 9 8 7 6 5 4 3 2 1

America's Publisher of Contemporary Romance

Printed in the U.S.A.

To my dear friend,
Teri Kovak Shapiro, who led the way

Time
Remembered

Chapter One

In the village of Sutton in New York's Dutchess County, that morning an early autumn breeze from the Hudson River played with the hem of Sabrina Burke's skirt as she watered the window boxes fronting the gray two-story clapboard house. The tabard sign that said SILVER BELLS & COCKLE SHELLS—*Antiques & Curios* swung gently above her head as she stepped back to admire the bright clusters of dwarf yellow chrysanthemums just coming into bloom. They gave new life to the century-old house that was Sabrina's home as well as her place of business.

The insistent clamor of the telephone inside the shop cut into the pleasure of the moment. Sabrina lingered dreamily, of half a mind to enjoy the morning's beauty a bit longer and let the darn phone ring, but it wasn't in her nature to do so. When the bell persisted she gave in to it, more out of habit than out of conscience.

"I'm coming. I'm coming," she muttered resentfully as she picked up the empty watering can. With a parting look at the autumn splendor around her, she reluctantly hurried in.

The cheerful tinkle from a cluster of silver bells that hung on the doorframe inside, a short time later warned Sabrina that the day's first customer had arrived a half hour before opening time.

"Oh, bother!" she murmured, remembering too late that she had forgotten to set the lock when she rushed inside to answer what had proved to be a wrong number.

Perched precariously on the top step of a kitchen ladder, she tried to pretend she had not heard the entry. She stretched a slender arm to reach the last of the store's seven antique clocks on a high shelf overlooking the store and gave its key a final turn. Still in her whim of self-indulgence, she did not turn around but waited for the next moment when all seven clocks began to chime the hour of nine. She could never get them to perform quite in unison but near enough to fill the room with music and her heart with delight.

So she had let an untimely customer slip in before she was ready . . . was it something to spoil her day?

She lingered a second longer to enjoy the fulfilling sounds. As the clocks played on, she turned dutifully at last to face the early visitor. When she saw it to be a tall, broad-shouldered man, she gave a small, involuntary gasp of surprise. Most of her clients were women, though they often brought husbands later to reject or pay for the articles selected by their wives.

She was there, poised for an instant as if suspended,

staring down at the newcomer, half-hypnotized by the magnetism of deep-set eyes as blue as a fathomless lake. He was much nearer the ladder than she had imagined before she turned to look. The nearness of the man took her breath away.

The eyes were what held her. Their blueness—so exceptionally dark under the craggy brow—was enhanced by a careless sweep of sable hair, like a splash of paint across the broad forehead, and by clear amber skin that searing rays of the sun would bronze but never burn. There was an aura of strength about the man that left no doubt in her mind that he would be dauntless and indestructible if brought to test.

As if in a dream, Sabrina took stock of the tall, splendidly balanced figure, the masterful lift of the head. Taken alone, his features might be considered homely, but together they composed a uniquely handsome face.

Under the steady gaze, Sabrina stepped forward—quite forgetting where she stood—and plunged headlong off the stepladder, landing in an ignominious heap on the floor at the newcomer's feet. In the next instant she felt the electric touch of his hand upon her shoulder and the hot blood rush to her face. She was appalled that the trembling within her might give her away.

"Are you all right?" a deep baritone voice above her asked.

She pulled herself together, uncomfortably aware that the hem of her sunburst-pleated skirt was halfway up to her waist, exposing an excessive length of body-stockinged legs. She twisted away from the hand that burned like a brand on her shoulder and scrambled to sit up, tucking her long legs hastily under the teal blue plaid of her skirt. Too shaken still to stand, she pushed the veil of ash-blond hair back from her face. Nearby the grandfather clock, the last of the seven to strike, gave a final "bong" for the hour of nine before Sabrina dared to lift her own blue eyes to meet those that looked down upon her.

He was on his knees beside her now, very close—so close she was sure he must sense how unnerved she was.

"Are you sure you're all right?" he insisted, a note of authority in his voice that brooked no nonsense.

Shaken though she was, Sabrina scampered to her feet, determined to make no more of a fool of herself than she'd already managed in the presence of the disturbing man.

"Quite sure," she said stiffly. She was dismayed to see the concern in his eyes turn to amusement as he rose to his feet beside her.

"A charming performance! Do you always welcome your customers with acrobatics and a fanfare of clocks?" he asked.

Sabrina's sense of decorum was shattered by the man's levity. She'd been lucky not to break her neck. The nerve of this—this *intruder,* making fun of her! Quickly she turned her head and walked away from him toward her private alcove at the rear of the store, tears of humiliation and anger scalding her eyes. She certainly didn't intend to provide the stranger further entertainment by letting him see her face in its disarray.

She spoke back over her shoulder, her voice tight as she fought for control. "I must ask you to leave," she said frostily. "The shop is not open for business until

9:30. You are welcome to come back then, if you care to."

He was probably not even a customer—at least not with money to spend. Maybe his wife had sent him to look for something better found in flea markets than in a collector's shop such as hers. His clothes might have come from a thrift shop, though the ancient jacket was of fine Harris tweed. It had taken the shape of the man, as had snug-fitting levis, laundry-faded and frayed but freshly clean. He wore a tattersall shirt with collar threadbare. Open halfway to the waist, it exposed a crop of darkish chest hair. What looked to be custom-made ankle-high walking boots were scarred by many miles of wear.

Still, he'd recently been to an expensive barber. One could never be sure in this day of casual dress. He might be a professor or an actor or a stockbroker or a millionaire. Or a bum. Or a confidence man.

She heard no sound of movement behind her as she walked away. When she reached the alcove, she turned to find the man standing where she had left him, boldly watching her retreat with no effort whatever to hide the fact. She should order him from the store, that's what she *should* do.

But the strange, deep blue eyes compelled hers, held them against her will. She had no voice to tell him to go.

Fighting for composure, Sabrina's anger was lost in a wave of electric excitement that seemed to come to her from out of his eyes. By a sheer act of will she looked away. Peripherally, she saw him shrug and move with an easy grace toward the front of the store. At the door he looked back and bowed slightly in a mocking parody of a formal leave-taking.

"I shall return," he intoned imperiously, his voice sustaining the parody. "May I suggest that in the meantime you lock your door, unless you really want to repeat that stellar performance for the next stray customer who wanders in before opening time."

He was gone.

She waited a moment now, half hoping the disturbing stranger would come back. Accepting at last that she waited in vain, she crossed back to the front door and reset the latch. She felt again the electric shock of the strong, yet gentle hand as it had reached her shoulder to help her up. Unexpectedly, a delicious shiver danced through her body.

How had she appeared to him, there on his knees beside her, so close that she could feel the heat of his body, his splendid maleness assaulting her every sense? She paused before a full-length mirror on a sidewall to look at herself with new eyes.

It had been a long time since Sabrina had given particular thought to her own looks. As a child the unfailing "Beauty is as beauty does," spoken chidingly by Aunt Hat whenever Sabrina had been told she was a "pretty child" had caused her to think of mere "prettiness" as more of a burden than she cared to endure.

Later, in her teens, she had felt a kind of transient gratitude—when she thought of the matter at all—that she strongly resembled her mother, a striking beauty even at the time of her death; rather than Aunt Hat, her father's sister, who was not. Still later, Sabrina shrugged away as simply a part of the dating game the extravagant compliments of a succession of young men who pursued her through college and whom she had refused to take seriously. They all seemed so aimless, so immature, so prone to grapple.

She lingered now before the looking glass and smoothed the soft blue-green cowl-necked sweater down over trim hips in their matching skirt and secured the catch on the narrow leather belt which had come unfastened in the fall, before taking stock. What she saw was a slender, full bosomed figure and above it the same fine oval face as her mother's; the peach-flower skin, the eyes of hyacinth blue.

She made her way to her private retreat through a maze of antiques and objects d'art, looking back on her part in the recent encounter with a certain ambivalence.

For all she knew, she had just lost a good customer a few minutes before by making a silly spectacle of herself. That hurt. But if a second meeting was not to be her fortune, at least there was some satisfaction in knowing that the legs the exciting stranger had glimpsed displayed in such unseemly manner, were shapely; the rest . . . well . . . *presentable*. Mirrored before her eyes she saw a picture she dared hope he would find hard to put out of his mind—might even lead him to return. Still, there was comfort to be had in knowing the legs she had displayed in an unseemly manner were shapely; and, as far as she could determine, there was nothing about her appearance that was likely to offend the eye.

Sabrina's hideaway was no more than a small corner set off from the rest of the shop by a splendid oriental screen, but she had a special fondness for this small domain. There she kept a few of her cherished belongings, the most precious of which was a small mahogany tambour desk that had belonged to her mother and before that to maternal grandmothers for more than a hundred years.

The desk was open now, and the hinged writing board let down as she had left it to accommodate a sheaf of inventory papers. She shuffled through them idly, with unseeing eyes, her thoughts still locked in the encounter with the remarkable man.

What strange wizardry had he worked on her that would make her imagine, now he was gone, that he was unlike any other man? It wasn't simply that he was handsome; there'd been handsome men in her life before. The thought brought her to her senses. How could she say he was "in her life" when he'd merely walked in and walked out again? "Passing through" was more like it.

Deep inside there stirred a poignant feeling of loss, but anger at her own skittish behavior as much as at the man surged up swiftly and drove the feeling away. Why had she made such a monkey of herself? She has swooned like a star-struck groupie over a total stranger. In all probability she had lost a customer for the store as well.

Aunt Hat—not even her mother—would have let a potential customer slip away through vain foolishness. The two genteel, valiant women had started the little antique-curio shop with family treasures after the death of Sabrina's father. The collapse of the Burke-Glendon fortunes and subsequent loss of Glenhaven, the old Tudor mansion on the Hudson which had been the home of Glendons since what seemed like the beginning of time, had left Sabrina's mother in dire financial straits. The combined instincts, judgment and impeccable taste of the two women in selecting replacements for family antiques and heirlooms, once these had been sold, earned the shop an enviable reputation long before it became Sabrina's to run.

Now it was hers, and she'd lost a customer through pure flightiness, one she wasn't apt to see on the premises again, nor soon erase from her mind. Her truant thoughts would not bow to the discipline of account books but skittered willfully away in fruitless imaginings. The figures before her eyes dissolved into a stunningly realized vision of her recent visitor.

What manner of man was he—this extraordinary male creature who forced himself upon her consciousness with an assurance just short of arrogance? Yet in the strongly chiseled face and deep-set eyes she had seen humor; sensed a fire of passion tempered with the grace of compassion.

With a sigh, she took up the inventory figures in earnest, checking them against books and billing sheets, grateful again that she had taken business training along with literature and art history courses at the expensive liberal arts college her mother and Aunt Harriet had sacrificed to send her to. It somehow assuaged a feeling she'd let them down; for she suspected she'd been sent there to make a good marriage as much as for anything.

Sometimes she wondered if she should have married one of the very eligible young men who had asked her while she was still in school. Certainly, she never wanted to go through life alone like her aunt, whose years of youth had slipped away as she devoted herself to Sabrina and her ailing mother. It saddened Sabrina that her aunt seemed likely now to live out her years with no more gratifying companion to share them with than her niece.

Lately Sabrina was tempted at times to give up and marry Ralph Spurling who had a good future in the insurance business and matrimony clearly in mind. He was handsome and agreeable enough. Still, the prospect of spending the rest of her life across the table from someone who talked largely about underwriting and mortality tables and the like depressed her somehow.

But it was more than that. Her real trouble, she knew, was that she had spent her whole life fantasizing about the man she would marry some day, and Ralph didn't fill the bill. She dreamed of a man she could thrill to, respect, admire; a man whose very presence would charge her with electric excitement, whose voice would fill her with joy. Secretly, deep inside, though she was ashamed to admit such a girlish notion, she liked to believe she would know him by the sound of bells in her heart.

A noise at the front door now brought her to her feet, pulse pounding, cheeks aflame. Oblivious to papers sent flying, she rushed around the screen and stopped sheepishly in her tracks at the sight of Ethel, one of two local women who worked the shop during the busy hours of the day, arriving with the morning mail.

"Morning, Sabrina. You got a card from your aunt."

Annoyed with herself, Sabrina took the mail and turned back to her alcove. What a fuss over a single lost customer! Angrily, she picked up the papers she had scattered across the floor.

The card from Aunt Hat was written at the Great Wall of China, one of her "I am fine wish you were here" cards that came regularly every week from wherever her aunt happened to find herself.

"I'm worn out running this place, Sabrina. It's all yours," her aunt had said to her that day after her graduation two years ago, two years after Sabrina's mother's death. "All my life I've wanted to see the world, and I'm going to do it."

Dear Aunt Hat! she thought, as out of the silence the first of the clocks began to chime the half hour. One by one the other six took up the tune. It was 9:30 A.M. Silver Bells & Cockle Shells was open for business, but of course he would not come back.

The shop was busy that morning. In addition to familiar faces—antique dealers, private collectors, knowledgeable housewives who regularly came to buy —there was an unusual number of strangers. These, for the most part, were city people out to catch the autumn color while the maples were in full blaze—strays from Route 9, the east Hudson thoroughfare a few miles away, in search of apples, antiques and artifacts to bear testimony that country folk, indeed, are quaint.

Her spirit sagged as she tried to adjust to a growing certainty she would not find herself in that splendidly pervasive male presence again.

When the hour of twelve was sung out by all seven clocks, and she had seen her last customer to the door, her assistant put on her jacket and started to leave.

"Wait Ethel," Sabrina called out on impulse from

her desk where she had gone back to her paper work. "Would you mind bringing me a sandwich when you come back from lunch?"

The woman looked at her young employer in surprise. This was not a run-of-the-day request. Sabrina's practice was to retreat to the other part of the house adjoining the shop which was her home, there to eat a lunch of her own making upon Ethel's return.

"Why of course," Ethel replied heartily after a moment of surmise. "What kind would you like me to bring?"

Under the older woman's curious eyes Sabrina felt her face go warm. "Oh, any kind. No—not tuna. Not—oh, bring me a Swiss cheese on rye and a carton of milk," she finished in a clumsy burst of words. Ethel, clearly puzzled, turned and went on her way.

Alone, Sabrina looked back on the moment in dismay. Now Ethel would wonder what had come over her. For that matter, so did she, herself. Suppose the man *did* come back and Sabrina happened to be eating lunch in the other part of the house, her presence would not be missed. Ethel was quite up to handling any sale in her absence.

In an act of self-punishment Sabrina opened a ledger and forced her attention on the columns of figures. Nevertheless, with the first jingle of silver bells over the front door she was on her feet, heart pounding furiously, senselessly in her breast. At the very moment she was about to rush forth she had more rational second thoughts and composed herself. A discreet peek around the Chinese screen acted upon her like a pinprick to a balloon.

It was not enough that the stranger who stood just inside the shop's entryway was not the one she'd been waiting for, it was a woman, a certain city type that Sabrina always found intimidating. It helped not at all to remind herself that bookfuls of words in praise of her own beauty had been poured in her ears all her life.

This woman was not even pretty. Below the smart, closely cropped curls, small eyes were made to appear larger by expertly applied liner and false lashes, but no makeup could disguise the aggressive thrust of her jaw.

In spite of her flaws, the woman was a model of cool sophistication in her high-heeled Ferregamo boots, wearing a pure silk blouse and a faultlessly tailored jacket with skin-tight designer jeans. There was an air of utter assurance about the woman that made nothing else count.

So much for beauty, thought Sabrina acidly as she steeled herself to plunge headlong into the patronizing presence awaiting her out there.

"May I help you," she asked.

The woman surveyed her coolly just long enough to leave Sabrina feeling dowdy and gauche before she said, "Not really, unless, of course, you are in charge."

"I own the shop," Sabrina replied, vainly trying to keep the pique from sounding in her voice.

With a jangle of gold bracelets the woman reached into her leather bag and brought out two cards—the first a smartly designed business card which read *Rhonda Bartlett, Interiors*, and below that a Manhattan address Sabrina recognized as Soho where it was currently chic to maintain a loft. The second card established Ms. Bartlett's credentials as a decorator.

"I'm up here to look at a place on the river to the north that a client of mine has bought. As long as I'm here I thought I might as well see what the local shopkeepers have to offer. If I run across anything I can use, we can expect the customary professional discount, of course."

It took all Sabrina's powers to keep her voice formally polite as she returned the cards to their bearer. "I can't speak for the rest of Sutton's stores, but here prices are the same for all buyers. This is a small, purely retail shop. Some of our fine antiques we have on consignment at their owner's asking price."

"I doubt the matter will come up. Offhand, I don't see anything I can't live without," said the decorator with a shrug. "If I find anything, we can negotiate." Without the courtesy of waiting for a rejoinder, she turned and walked rudely away.

Sabrina's mind turned ruefully back to her first visitor of the day. For a moment she stopped still and let herself drown once more in the memory of dark pools of indigo eyes. With a sigh she put the image, along with her present annoyance, behind her. Reminding herself she must take the bad with the good, she hurried to greet two newly arrived visitors, pleased to recognize them both as frequent buyers whom she looked upon as old friends.

She was in the midst of a discussion of a small Hepplewhite chair with a patron a short time later when a demanding voice called out from her private corner behind the oriental screen, a rude reminder of the unwelcome presence in the store.

Sabrina stopped in mid-sentence, scarcely able to believe her ears. Turning toward the sound, she was annoyed to see Rhonda Bartlett step out from behind the screen.

"Miss—Ms.—*Madame Proprietor*—whatever you answer to, will you kindly come here?" The voice of the decorator, while not actually loud, was clear to Sabrina as if there were no other sounds in the store.

"Would you please excuse me for a moment," she said to her customer.

The decorator had stepped back behind the screen when Sabrina reached the spot, a possessive hand planted firmly on the little tambour desk, clearly determined to hold the floor.

"I'll take this desk," she announced.

"The desk is not for sale," said Sabrina shortly. Then in her most formal voice, "I must ask you to step back into the salesroom. This part of the shop is private. There's nothing here to be sold."

It was as if the woman heard no more than the first words. "Don't be silly! Of course the desk is for sale."

"Indeed it is not," said Sabrina firmly. "The desk is my personal property. I have no intention of selling it."

"My dear Ms.—by the way, darling, what *is* your name?" The decorator's whole demeanor had changed. Now the arrogant voice dripped honey and at the same time was insufferably patronizing.

"Burke," snapped Sabrina.

"Thank you. Now, Ms. Burke, I presume you are in business to make money, just like everyone else in the world. I'm in a position to pay you a great deal for this desk."

"It is not for sale," said Sabrina stubbornly.

"Be reasonable. It is exactly what I want for a particular bay-windowed study that looks out over the river in this place I'm about to do. I might even find a few other pieces here that I could make do, if you could see your way clear to let me have this desk."

Sabrina scarcely heard the last words. Her breath caught in her throat. *Bay-windowed study—looks out over the river.* Could it be the room that had been her mother's personal nook at Glenhaven? Half fearing the answer, she had to ask.

"The house—the one your client bought—it wouldn't be Glenhaven, by any chance?"

"House? Oh, the one I came up to see?" said Ms. Bartlett, clearly growing impatient. "Locally it's known as Glenhaven, I believe; but really, Ms. Burke, that has nothing to do with the desk."

So the old family home had again changed hands, thought Sabrina. In answer to the decorator, she replied, "There's nothing more to be said about the desk."

The woman snatched up her expensive bag from the chair where she had let it drop and started around the screen. A few steps out, she turned back.

"Don't think I don't know your game! You think you can gouge me for twice what the desk is worth if you hold out." With that for a parting shot, the decorator made for the door to the street, the high stacked leather heels of her boots sounding in a fast percussion across the hardwood floor.

Chapter Two

"You look kinda peaky, Sabrina," Ethel observed when she arrived back from lunch shortly, bringing with her Sabrina's other helper, Dora, with whom she had just had lunch. "It's such a pretty day, why don't you take your sandwich and the dog and go down to the river for a walk. It's not going to stay nice like this for long."

Sabrina hesitated. "It's been a hectic morning, Ethel. It could get even worse this afternoon. I hate to leave you alone," she demurred.

"Don't worry about it. It's not Dora's day, but she'll stick around just in case, won't you Dora?"

It took no more than Dora's amiable nod to send Sabrina on her way. Her heart suddenly lighter, she caught up the brown bag Ethel had brought her and slipped into a camel-colored cardigan. She hurried out through the kitchen in the other part of the house to get her walking companion, Hero, the dog.

The golden retriever was a gift from Aunt Hat who feared for her niece's safety on the long river walks Sabrina often took, but as a guard dog, it developed, he left much to be desired. A quiet creature who seldom barked, he adored people indiscriminately, refused to take Sabrina's mild disciplinary efforts seriously and was an incurable escape artist.

Dropping to her knees, Sabrina hugged the fine russet head to her body as she fastened his collar and leash. The plumey tail beat a tattoo on the rough tile floor in delight at the prospect of a romp.

It was one of those warm, hazy autumn days with the scent of woodsmoke in the air when the whole world seemed on fire with color, and she turned her steps to Glenhaven, wondering how much longer she'd have the run of its grounds. Mr. Speers, who bought the estate out of receivership, gave a key to the gate and an open invitation to walk there whenever they liked to her aunt and mother long ago. As far as Sabrina knew, neither had ever gone back; but she loved its labyrinthine river paths, and even though it had become overgrown with brush and littered with wind-fallen limbs, it was her favorite walking grounds.

The golden-red dog trotted docilely along beside her now on his leash and stood at attention while she slipped her key in the lock of the big double gate, relieved to find that the new owner had not yet changed locks.

Once inside, Hero leaned impatiently against the leash and pulled her jerkily along, a few steps at a time. Sabrina held back to turn her eyes up to the big three-story fieldstone mansion built nearly two hundred years before by a direct ancestor of her mother's, Edward Glendon, who made his fortune in early day shipping.

It was not so extravagantly grand as the mansion built down the river a few years later by Frederick Vanderbilt nor did it have the rambling robustness of the well-lived-in, thirty-room Hyde Park home of the Roosevelts nearby. Still Glenhaven, even in its present state of dilapidation, had an elegant grace, a decaying, yet dignified charm.

It was indeed dilapidated. Because of a family illness, Mr. Speers had become an absentee owner in recent years, leaving an aging caretaker to see to the upkeep of the big house and grounds. Inevitably, as time went on, the house had fallen into disrepair, and the plantings had grown into a jungle of underbrush.

Sabrina's favorite fantasy, as a teenager, was of sudden fortune which would buy back the estate and turn it again into the showplace it had been in her parents' time.

She turned away from the house now and let herself be pulled headlong down the path past the carriage house and a weathered bench placed where the grounds began their slope to the river, and where she had thought to eat her lunch, all the way to the bottom. There the ground leveled out into a rampant growth of brush and saplings.

Wading through wild asters and waist-high goldenrod in full bloom so tall they hid old railroad tracks that ran parallel to the river, she came upon a small clearing where a tree had fallen and another fallen across it. These formed an inviting seat where she could still eat her lunch at an elevation high enough to see out over the brush to the broad, swiftly flowing waters of the Hudson.

Off the leash Hero deserted her, bounding away through the brush; leaving Sabrina to perch on the crossed logs and eat her Swiss cheese sandwich on rye.

Gazing out at the dark water, she wondered if this would be her last visit to this beloved woodland spot. One could hardly blame the new owner if he didn't care to have the orphan of former owners trailing ghosts of the past across his grounds.

The snap of a limb behind her startled Sabrina from her thoughts and brought her around, a greeting on her lips for the big golden dog. The words froze on her tongue.

There, only a few feet away, creeping stealthily up on her came a big, red-eyed, unshaven mongrel of a person, dressed in a dirty windbreaker and baggy brown pants. Sabrina gave a small cry of alarm. The evil-looking character lunged forward and made a grasp for her arm, but she managed to elude him. At the same time she opened her mouth and screamed at the top of her lungs. The next moment he caught her around the neck in an iron grip and clapped a dirty hand over her mouth.

"Shut up!" he ordered, giving vent to a string of obscenities. "Shut up and gimme your money, you won't get hurt, but bygod you will if you holler again."

With the dirty hand pressed hard against her mouth the terrified Sabrina could not explain she never carried a purse when she was out for a walk. Sizing up the situation, the assailant spat out a vicious oath and grabbed the chain from which hung her grandmother's lovely gold watch and jerked it violently. It held firm. Again and again he yanked. Each time the chain cut into her flesh until she feared her neck would be broken before the chain. At last, to her relief, the chain came apart. Stuffing the watch and chain in a pocket, the attacker grabbed her arm and stripped from it an old-fashioned bracelet of braided gold.

The only other thing of value Sabrina wore was an heirloom gold and pearl ring which fit so snugly it was hard to remove. She was too nearly paralyzed with fear of what the villain might do when he'd taken the last of her valuables to feel pain as he tugged viciously at her finger.

The ring gave way, but as he pocketed it a deep, forceful voice roared out suddenly from the slope behind them, "Let go of her at once!"

The marauder let go of Sabrina and took off in a lumbering run.

Sabrina's legs buckled and, as a figure flashed by her, she fell to her knees. In paralyzed fascination, she watched a big, splendidly coordinated male body fly through the air in a perfect flying tackle and nail the escaping assailant to the ground.

With his quarry pinned down, Sabrina's rescuer turned his head to look back at her with concern. From where she knelt, her whole body trembling in aftershock, she looked across the space into the rough hewn face of her morning visitor. The man had shed his coat and was in shirt sleeves now. The sinews of his upper arms rippled with power as he held down his struggling prey.

"You okay?" he called out above an outburst of gross expletives from his captive which he cut short by the

29

simple expedient of pressing the villain's face into the ground.

Sabrina nodded, but it was a moment before she could speak. "Okay—fine—" Her words quavered in spite of herself.

"You're sure you're not hurt?"

She shook her head, too near tears of relief to risk her voice again.

He watched her anxiously for a moment. "Stay where you are. When you feel up to it, toss me your scarf. I may need it to tie his hands so I can get him some place to turn him over to the police," he said. Lifting his prisoner's head by the hair to let him breathe once more, he advised the surly creature grimly, "If you want to keep on breathing, don't let me hear a word from that foul mouth of yours."

Before the problem of disposing of the miscreant could be dealt with, Sabrina glanced up to see Hero bounding through the woods a short distance ahead of her, two uniformed policemen a few steps behind. It was she the officers saw first as Hero frisked over to the crossed logs where she had seated herself, still trembling too much to stand.

"You'd better take your dog and get out of here, lady," one of the officers called out. "This is no place for you. We got a tip that an escaped prisoner had been—oh, my—!" he broke off as his eyes fell on the scene beyond her for the first time.

As the two rushed forward Sabrina saw her rescuer get to his feet to let the armed officers take charge. Before her horrified eyes the prisoner seized the moment to come up behind him, wielding a piece of fallen limb as big around as a man's arm and some three feet long. As the villain swung his truncheon directly at the head of his erstwhile captor Sabrina screamed. Warned, the man ducked and lunged, bringing the fugitive down for the second time with a low tackle. There he stayed until securely handcuffed by one of the officers, who pulled him to his feet and patted him down for weapons.

Except for a wing of dark hair across his forehead and a certain amount of rubble still caught on his clothes, Sabrina's rescuer appeared as cool and unruffled as if the whole fracas had been rehearsed. While the older of the two officers searched their captive, he stood off to the side talking to the younger one. In a moment the two broke off their conversation to come to where Sabrina sat, still too shaken to join them. As they approached she got to her feet unsteadily, supporting herself against a sapling, afraid to trust herself to move.

"Did he take anything from you, by any chance, ma'am?" the officer asked.

"Yes! I almost forgot," she gasped. "A ring and a bracelet and my grandmother's watch."

"That's all he had on him," said the officer when she had described the pieces to his satisfaction and returned them to her. "Luckily, he'd just been arrested during the night so his gun's at the station, but he's a bad egg even without it. You'd have been in big trouble if this man hadn't happened to drive in at the right moment. He heard you scream as he got out of his car."

"Where did he—that terrible person—come from?" Sabrina asked.

"Well, ma'am, he broke out of the local lockup before we could get him moved to the county jail," the young policeman said with a sheepish grin.

The officer guarding the prisoner and at the same time operating a walkie-talkie device to the outside, signaled his companion to come.

As they started off with their shackled prisoner, the young officer called back to them, "Would it be too much trouble for you folks to stay right here for a few minutes? We'll take this fellow to a squad car out on the highway. Then I'd like to ask you a few questions for my report."

Sabrina looked around at the scene of the scramble, averting her eyes quickly from the handcuffed captive. She gave an involuntary shudder and turned pleading eyes up to the man who stood at her side. As if he sensed and understood her reluctance to stay, he came to her rescue again.

"There's a bench at the top of the bank, near the carriage house, officer. We'll wait for you there," he called back.

In a moment the two officers and their prisoner had disappeared over the crest of the sloping bank.

In the sudden silence, Sabrina drew a quavering breath and ventured a step forward away from the supporting sapling. In a delayed reaction, her whole body began to tremble again like the leaves on an aspen tree. Had the man not reached out and steadied her, she would have fallen to her knees again.

"I was so afraid," she whispered. "Thank heavens you came."

He engulfed her in his arms and held her quietly, running a comforting hand across her shoulders, softly stroking the pale gold head buried against the bulwark of his muscular chest. Her trembling gradually subsided, and she smiled up at the man weakly, startled again at the incredible dark blue eyes so near to her.

"I'm all right now. Thanks."

"Wait a minute! Let's take a look at these welts." The dark head bent nearer. Strong, gentle fingers touched the fiery lacerations at her throat. "I should have broken his neck," he muttered grimly. "Does it hurt much?"

"Not now," she replied, for in truth, her only sense was of the touch of his hand at the base of her throat. The hand came away. She shuddered slightly. "Let's get out of here, please."

Before she could move he swept her, protesting, off her feet and carried her swiftly up the slope to the weathered bench in his arms. There he set her down and dropped to the ground at her feet. They rested for a moment in the tenuous silence that often follows a shared moment of high drama, the majestic river before them; behind them, the great house. Hero gamboled about them happily as if they were all players in some mysterious but interesting game in which he did not fully understand his part. After a moment the man's eyes turned up to Sabrina, assessing her with concern.

"Thanks again," she said with a still shaky smile. "After my rudeness at the shop this morning you had every right to leave me to fend for myself." She was surprised to see a glint of curiosity in the deep-set eyes.

"Well, I did barge in on you before opening time."

"Oh, people do it all the time. I don't really mind, except when I go flying off a ladder at their feet. It was

33

my shattered vanity that made me snappish, I'm afraid," she admitted sheepishly. "Please accept my apology."

"Vanity? Is *that* all? I was afraid I was a reminder of something you preferred to forget. Truth is, you made my day," he said with a laugh.

Though the reply surprised her, the warm laughter filled her with unexpected delight. A kind of companionable weariness, as if they waited for a second wind, settled over the two of them and wrapped them again in a comfortable silence. The golden retriever, tired of the game, curled up at Sabrina's feet, and the big man's hand reached out to scratch the dog's ears. Hero inched closer to rest his head on the flexed knee.

After a time the man asked, "Do you come here often?"

"Oh yes. It's my favorite walking spot," she told him. "Unfortunately, since Mr. Speers, the owner, moved away it has turned into a regular jungle; but the dog loves it." Again she gave a little involuntary shiver. "I may decide to confine my walks to the Vanderbilt place and Hyde Park. They're not so conveniently located, but one's hardly likely to get mugged."

The deep blue eyes of her rescuer gazed across the sun-dappled river as if looking into another world.

"This used to be my favorite spot, too, when I was a kid," he said quietly. "Dad bought me a spyglass, and I had a crows nest up in one of those big trees where I watched the ships come up the river."

Sabrina looked at him curiously. "Then you must be a relative of Mr. Speers," she said.

He looked at her in surprise. "No. I'm Jules Danner.

I guess because I know you are Sabrina Burke, I took it for granted you knew."

The name stirred troubled recollections. A sudden uneasiness settled over Sabrina.

"You—you are a relative of my father's partner, Archibald Danner?"

"His son," Danner replied. "I played here at Glenhaven ten years before you were born and a few years after; but until I came back recently I hadn't been here for years. I graduated from college in California and stayed out there. The call of the Hudson brought me back."

His answer disturbed Sabrina and put her suddenly at a loss. What she knew about the Danner-Burke relationship was so vague, so nebulous, she had no idea what was appropriate for her to say now to this man who stirred her so.

"By the way," Danner said when she made no response, "the reason I dropped in at your shop this morning was to take a look at little Sabrina Burke after seventeen years, but it seemed not a propitious time to tell you so."

Sabrina struggled to compose herself. For her, the warm feeling of companionship had dissolved. She felt a desperate need to break the growing silence between them but, for the life of her, couldn't come up with a thing to say.

The red-gold dog raised up in a sudden move to take off. Danner pressed him down again with a firm hand, at the same time ordering him to stay. Hero eyed the big man for a moment, as if to make sure he meant it, before settling back, but not until he had given the hand that disciplined him a respectful lick.

Sabrina ventured a cautious question. "What brings you back to Glenhaven?"

"I bought it. About six weeks ago."

Sabrina's eyes widened in stunned surprise, and her sense of impending disaster mounted. If Jules Danner had the money to buy Glenhaven, the Danners had survived the fatal crash of the partnership far better than the Burkes. Her voice, when she spoke, was unexpectedly shaky once more.

"You are living here?"

"Not yet. The house is badly run down. I've hired an architect. Meanwhile, there's an apartment over the carriage house I had renovated," he said. "I'm living there."

"But how can that be possible? Why haven't I seen you here before—or your car?"

"That's not surprising," he assured her. "My business is in Poughkeepsie. I've been in and out a lot since I came. It would be more surprising, actually, for you to run into me here." He laid a hand on the big dog's head. "Now, this fellow, I know."

"Hero?"

Danner grinned and nodded ruefully. "I've given him a few rides to the animal shelter, in fact. He's popped in here when I was around and the gate was open. Once I drove up and found him waiting for me to open the gate."

"He's a terrible tramp," she murmured distractedly. "He runs away every chance he gets. I didn't realize he came here."

"If your name had been on his collar, I would have delivered him to you personally but I didn't know who he belonged to."

Except on the surface, Sabrina's mind was far away from the dog. Questions that had laid dormant most of her adult life had suddenly begun to roil within her. As if they would no longer remain unspoken, they poured out—almost against her will—words tumbling over each other as out of a cask when the stopper has been pulled.

"Tell me about my father—the partnership—the Burkes and the Danners," she begged. "What was that all about?"

The deep-set eyes were suddenly inscrutable. It was as if a door had been slammed in her face. With a sharp order for the golden retriever to stay, Jules Danner got to his feet. He turned away from Sabrina to look out at the river.

From over his shoulder he asked brusquely, "Just how much do you know?"

"Only that everything went down the tube for some reason." She tried to speak lightly but a slight break in her voice as she went on gave her away. "It was all very painful for my mother, and she never was well, so—well, we just didn't talk about it—ever. The whole subject was taboo."

A change had come over Jules Danner. She saw a look of evasion in the deep blue eyes before he turned away that hadn't been there before; and when he spoke again now it was without turning back to face her.

"And your father? Do you remember your father at all?"

"Of course. I was already five when he died. I remember him as a gentle, sensitive man who wrote wonderful stories and poems for me and painted charming watercolor landscapes that hang on the walls of my room at home," she said. "But that doesn't tell me a thing about the business or the partnership. What happened? What went wrong?"

The uneasy silence once more enveloped them. From the weathered bench where she sat, Sabrina watched the strong masculine back, the fine broad shoulders, the wind-roughened sweep of sable hair with a sense of bewilderment and a tug at her heart. What had she done to chill the warmth she had felt growing between them? She got to her feet and crossed the few steps to stand beside him, shoulder high next to the tall, brooding man.

"Please tell me," she said. "There's no one else I can ask."

He looked down at her then, tight-faced, the deep eyes telling her nothing at all.

"I was just a kid myself. I don't know any more about it than you," he told her harshly. There was an uncharacteristic note of self-consciousness in the abrasive voice that left her no doubt he lied.

For a moment she was about to challenge him. Then down the driveway that led across the grounds to the river came the police car, wheeling in beside Danner's cream-colored Mercedes in front of the carriage house nearby. The officer who had asked them to wait stepped out.

It took but a few minutes for him to get answers to all pertinent questions and fill out necessary forms. When it appeared the officer was about to leave, Danner turned to Sabrina.

"Give me the leash, and I'll put it back on the dog," he said. "You'd be a bit crowded in my sports car with that big animal breathing down your neck, if I were to take you. The officer will see you home."

"I should say not!" Sabrina cried indignantly, furious at the high-handed way Danner foisted her off on the policeman. "I'm quite all right. Hero and I'll walk home."

"Nonsense," said Danner impatiently. He picked up the leash from the bench where she had left it. Snapping it to Hero's collar, he led the dog to the police car and ordered him into the back seat. Sabrina watched in helpless outrage.

"Mr. Danner's right, ma'am," the officer said. "You've had quite a shock. I'll be glad to drive you home."

Unyielding, Danner waited at the car door to escort her into the front seat. "Come, Sabrina. Get in," he ordered in much the same tone that had sent the dog lumbering into the back. If she didn't obey, would he pick her up bodily and dump her in? With a weary shrug of her shoulders, Sabrina did as she'd been told.

There was no way a person could be brought home in a police car without the whole world knowing, Sabrina thought crossly after a third non-buyer had dropped in "just browsing," and she had been obliged to repeat the story of her misadventure to each one.

"From now on, you tell it," she said at last to Ethel and Dora and retreated to her screened alcove leaving the two to deal with customers and curious as well.

In the silence of her own company, the burning pain of the raw welts on her neck brought the early afternoon's encounters back to her far more vividly than her own spoken words. Try as she might to settle down to her accounts, she found herself staring off into space, a rich baritone voice murmuring seductively in her head. The columns of figures dissolved into fleeting images of Jules Danner—the splendid masculine body, the commanding presence; the dark, unyielding eyes; all overshadowed by the compelling mystery of sudden change that came over Jules Danner when she asked direct questions about their fathers' ill-fated partnership.

Up to that moment she had basked in the warmth of their expanding relationship; then, unexpectedly, the chill. She felt again the shock of his sudden withdrawal, the certainty she had been callously thrust aside. Just as surely as he had tackled her assailant, Jules Danner had straight-armed her away from hidden secrets in his mind.

As business tapered off in the shop in the late afternoon, Sabrina restlessly pushed the ledger aside and went back into the salesroom to find it so quiet she soon sent Ethel and Dora home.

In the sudden silence after their departure the veil she had drawn over the pains and pleasures of her encounters with Jules Danner fell away. She caught her breath and forgot to breathe again as she relived the moment she lay cradled in his arms so short a time before, her head pressed against the broad chest as he bore her, trembling, and helpless, up the embankment. She felt the power and heat of his body, her nostrils quivering again to its seductive male aroma—and moaned inwardly as the silver bells over the door heralded a customer and wrenched her from her yearning reprise.

Alone again, a sale accomplished, she went grimly

back to her bookkeeping, determined to stick to the finish and allow no further indulgence in adolescent fantasies to interfere.

Finished at last, she stood up and stretched. As she moved her head back and forth to ease the tension in the back of her neck, she remembered she hadn't checked the gate after the trashman that afternoon. If Hero found it ajar, she wouldn't see him again until he turned up at the animal shelter—or worse, in the hands of Jules Danner at Glenhaven.

It wasn't the running away that bothered her so much as the dog's indifference to the perils of highways and streets, Sabrina thought as she hurried out to check the gate. If she didn't find a way to thwart the wayward beast, sooner or later he would get himself killed.

Finding the gate securely latched and Hero asleep in one corner of the yard, she lingered on the patio, relaxing for the first time all afternoon in the sun. Her peace was soon shattered by the sound of voices from within the store, and she remembered she had left the place wide open when she went flying out to look at the gate.

Hurrying across the kitchen, she was about to step through the door into the shop when something familiar in the voice that was speaking caused her to hesitate and listen.

"Can you believe it, Silver Bells and Cockle Shells!" the voice was saying on a derisive note. "But don't let the cutesy name mislead you. The place is simply a gold mine of antiques, darling. I must have found at least ten pieces this morning that I can use."

It was, of course, Ms. Bartlett, the decorator; and

with a companion, unless the woman talked to herself. Sabrina breathed a sigh of resignation. With the possibility of selling even three out of the ten pieces mentioned, she'd have to force herself to be gracious. Deep within, the voice of conscience reminded her that eavesdropping was a shabby trick which she would be ashamed of later. Still, the fact she would otherwise never have known what the decorator had in her mind kept Sabrina at her listening post as the voice moved nearer.

"But you must see this tambour desk, back here behind the screen. There's one almost like it at the White House," the decorator, in the alcove now, was saying just beyond the door. "Look Jules. Isn't it absolutely divine! You watch. She'll sell it to me, but it's going to take your help."

Jules? Jules Danner, of course, here with Glenhaven's decorator, thought Sabrina. Well, she had news for Mr. Danner. The desk was not for sale, not even to go back to Glenhaven. With her hand on the doorknob she was about to step out and get the fact established at once when the man spoke for the first time. His voice stayed her hand.

"Rhonda, my love, the desk appears to be in use," Jules Danner said chidingly. "You just don't do accounts on a desk that's up for sale."

"Nonsense, darling. Of course *she* says it's not for sale, but that's where you come in. You're going to turn on the full force of your masculine charm and tell her the desk is for you." The decorator's tone was like maple syrup. "She'll not only sell it, she'll give me the discount I ask."

The man gave a hoot of laughter. "Well, I'll say this

for you, Rhonda, baby. No one's about to lose money betting on your talent for buying to your own advantage, nor your lack of scruples when it's something you're out to get."

"That's why you can't do without me, angel," "Rhonda baby" purred, her words followed by a soft *whoosh* that sounded like nothing but a kiss.

Client! Sabrina exploded silently. Future Mrs. Jules Danner was more like it. *Darling . . . Angel . . . Rhonda, my love!* She had been pretty stupid to chalk off their use of the terms to the current fashion of endearments-for-everyone. No wonder the woman was determined to have the tambour desk, knowing all the time that the bay-windowed study was destined to be hers.

The picture of Rhonda Bartlett in her mother's window at her mother's desk was more than Sabrina could bear. About to burst in and confront the intruders, she reconsidered. She'd be darned if she would let them know she had been listening.

Silently she moved back across the kitchen to the outside door which she banged loudly. She then walked across the room in a purposeful, rather louder than usual stride to open the door to the shop and step across the threshold into the space directly in front of the desk. The two stood next to the Chinese screen. Sure enough, there was a smudge of scarlet lipstick on Jules Danner's cheek. Sabrina did not wait for either to speak.

"Apparently I did not make myself clear this morning, Ms. Bartlett. This area is open by invitation only, except for myself and my staff," she said with chilled politeness, astonished at her own icy control. Whatever sales it might cost her were well lost, she thought. "Now will you kindly get out of here and not trespass behind my screen again?"

Rhonda Bartlett left her tall companion and stepped aggressively into the sanctum. For the second time she placed a possessive hand on the desk, as if somehow Sabrina were the interloper. From below false lashes that extended out over her eyes like awnings the woman darted a glance at Danner and prompted him sweetly, "You tell her, darling—tell her you want the desk."

Humor twitched a corner of the man's mouth. He did not comply but watched curiously. When he made no move to break the growing silence, Ms. Bartlett insisted crossly, "Mr. Danner wants the desk."

"The desk is not for sale," Sabrina repeated wearily. She was heartily sick of the whole repetitious scenario and determined to put an end to it, whatever the cost in sales. "Now, I must insist you move into the salesroom. If there's anything there you want, you are welcome to it as long as you pay the price you will find clearly marked on each tag."

She was acutely aware of Jules Danner standing at the edge of the alcove watching the scene between the two women with a look of sardonic amusement that infuriated her. She felt her face go hot, but there was ice in her voice as she finished what she had started to say. With a sweep of her hand toward the rest of the store she said, "Out there, and for my price! My shop is a place of business, not a court where games are played."

Tossing Sabrina a wicked grin, Danner grasped the decorator by an elbow and steered her away from the desk. In the main shop, he turned to Sabrina. His amusement only partially concealed, he said straight-faced, "I'm relieved to see the day's misadventures left you with nothing worse than a bad temper and a bruised neck."

Sabrina's hand flew to her throat. She heard Ms. Bartlett mutter balefully for Jules Danner's ears alone, "Thanks for nothing! Next time I'll just walk in and take the blasted desk."

Her words brought an ironic chuckle from the man's throat, a new glint of laughter to the eyes. "You *are* a bit casual about locking that door," he said to Sabrina in a lightly goading tone.

Sabrina jumped to her defense. "The gate—," she began and thought, *oh, what's the use!*

At that moment the clocks chimed out the opening notes for the hour of five. As the full, combined chorus took over, Danner darted an audacious smile at Sabrina. His deep, musical voice rose above the harmony of the clocks as he took the decorator's arm again. "Come Rhonda. I think they're *all* asking us to leave," he said.

With a backward glance over his shoulder as he closed the door behind them, Jules Danner ushered the troublesome Ms. Bartlett from the store.

The gleam of mocking laughter in the eyes of the man was enraging. Sabrina trembled inside, out of sheer frustration. She waited a moment to make sure they had gone before going to the door to lock up, although it was still a half hour until closing time.

She leaned her aching head against the door panel and for a moment gave in to a hollow feeling that someone important had just walked in and out of her life; and nothing for her would ever be the same.

Chapter Three

If it had entered her mind at all, Sabrina would have thought of herself as a normally cheerful person not given to moods—and so she was. Still, as the week moved on she felt depressed. She worked with a restless fervor in the shop all day and at night slept fitfully.

Her dreams were full of weird journeys through the halls and chambers of Glenhaven or strange encounters with the shadowy figure of a strong, tall man whose indigo eyes held her under a Svengali sort of spell. Sometimes it was the tambour desk he shouldered and carried off; sometimes Sabrina, herself. In either case, in the dream, she was quite helpless to act contrary to his will.

Awakening early, her mind in turmoil from the disturbing dreams, she would put on a pair of sturdy walking shoes, dress warmly against the chill of the autumn dawn and, snapping a leash on Hero, set off on a brisk morning walk across private land, the plumey-tailed dog at her side.

Sabrina never thought of what she did as trespassing. For generations the families who had built these estates had been friends of her own family. Two of the properties—the Roosevelt and Vanderbilt places, which she particularly loved—had been given to the government years before as historic sites and were open a good part of most days to the public anyhow; their walkways overseen by Department of Interior guards and guides.

Toward the end of the week one morning, with the red-gold dog bounding along at her side, Sabrina walked at a swift clip all the way to Hyde Park, where Franklin Roosevelt spent much of his boyhood. Its easy-sloping wooded banks were netted with delightful paths on which Sabrina's own grandmother had played with Roosevelt children two generations earlier.

There she followed a path to the river and let Hero off his leash. After a first foray into the woods, the dog came back, and the two walked on companionably together. Suddenly the animal took off through the trees again with a purposefulness in his departure that made her uneasy. She called out to summon him back.

The big dog played deaf. He kept right on going, disappearing quickly in the woods, his red-gold coat a perfect camouflage against the autumn scene. Still calling, Sabrina hurried along the path in search of him. As it became apparent she might very well call herself hoarse, and her voice alone would not bring him back, she grew increasingly worried. Though Hero left much to be desired in the way of obedience, it was unlike him to desert her as he now seemed to have done.

Dropping down to the railroad tracks that ran along the bank, she plodded over ties for a distance, hoping the creature might spot her from the woods above and choose to come back on his own. When this too soon appeared to be a futile exercise, she concluded the only sensible course was to turn back for home and notify the animal shelter that her truant was again on the loose. On the verge of doing just that, she came in sight of a narrow grassy stretch. What she saw there stopped her short in astonishment, her pulse playing a quick grace note to its normal beat.

At the near end of the strip of green stood Jules Danner, the wind from the river ruffling his hair. Back turned to her, he looked off into the woods—tall, broad-shouldered, lazily relaxed.

She had not yet seen this remarkable man for the first time a week ago, she thought with a rush of breathless excitement. Now he was popping up everywhere. Quite forgetting that their earlier meetings had ended uncomfortably for her in every instance, she quickened her step and was about to call out when out of the woods came bounding the big red-gold dog. Her thrill of excitement dissolved into indignation as she saw that the beast carried a stick in his mouth which he brought to Danner, relinquishing it to his hand.

They were playing games!

With a small, lazy movement of his arm, Danner sent the stick flying again, and the dog charged off to fetch it.

"Hero!" she called out furiously when the wretch

48

emerged from the trees, bearing the stick. Again she called, only to be ignored as the dog went about his business of delivering his prize to the man, who turned his head to see where her voice was coming from as he reached for the stick.

Speechless with anger, Sabrina ran forward. Jules, seeing her, dropped the stick and came to meet her, Hero trotting amiably at his side. She stopped and waited, catching her breath while she prepared a cool speech to let Jules Danner know how annoyed she was with them both. It was a speech she was never permitted to deliver.

"I thought you had learned your lesson at Glenhaven the other day," Danner greeted her scathingly as he approached.

Surprised to find herself on the defensive, Sabrina could do no better than gasp, "What on earth are you doing here?"

"Revisiting boyhood haunts," replied Danner shortly. "Don't you ever keep this animal on the leash?"

"Of course!" Sabrina defended with asperity. "I always unsnap the leash down here along the river where it's wild. There are so few other places he can run free."

"Well don't do it. Here, of all places, keep the dog at your side," Danner ordered sharply, as if he had a right to tell her what to do. "I should think your experience the other day—"

"It's not the same at all," Sabrina interrupted crossly. "This is government property, and there are guides and guards all over the place. No escaped criminal is about to pick a spot like this to hide out."

"Don't count on it. Incidentally, escaped criminals

49

are only one of the potential dangers you could run across. There's no screening of visitors, you know."

"Are you trying to make me paranoid? Hero's a big dog, and he needs to run," she argued stubbornly.

Danner glared at her. "If you're going to be so foolhardy, don't expect me to rescue you again," he warned, and at the same time reached out and, in one quick, singularly effortless movement pulled her forward and turned her around facing out, locking her to him in a vise-like grip.

"What are you going to do now?" he goaded her grimly. Furious, she struggled to get away and found she was pinned fast.

"Where are your guards and guides now?" jeered Danner. The arrogance of the man's actions and words fanned the flame of anger that flickered within, yet Sabrina was enough of a realist to recognize when she was out-maneuvered and out-talked and soon left off struggling. She was at once burningly conscious of her body pressed against his.

As abruptly as he had seized her, Danner turned her around to face him, one strong arm still holding her tightly so it was impossible to pull away. The other hand tipped her face up, forcing her to look into the dark, volcanic eyes.

"Promise me you won't come down here along the river again with this animal off the leash," he ordered sternly.

"I'll do no such thing," snapped Sabrina. "The dog needs to run. He'd never attack a person, anyhow; so what difference does it make? I wouldn't want a dog that would."

"That's not the point," Danner said, his voice impatient. "Simply having him with you is protection enough. Nobody's going to attack someone who walks with a dog, particularly one as big as your Hero." While she didn't answer, he continued to tilt her face up, his own face still severe but with a suggestion of warmth in his eyes.

"Promise me, Sabrina!" Leaning down to her, he kissed her mouth lightly. Her heart thumped fiercely in her breast. He kissed her again, soundly this time, and let her go. Too stunned to speak, she stood frozen where he released her.

"All right, Princess, lecture's over," he said with a half smile. "I'm not out to get your back up. It's that the little girl of eighteen years ago has grown into a delightful spunky young woman. I shouldn't like to see her get hurt."

Sabrina dropped her eyes, suddenly unable to meet his gaze.

"We seem to have a faculty for getting off on the wrong foot," Jules said quietly after a moment. "If we try again, do you think we could be friends?"

Such a mixture of emotions churned within Sabrina she found it hard to compose herself for a reply. "How can you speak of friendship?" she asked finally, over her wildly beating heart. "Friends are open with each other, but when I asked you a question that mattered to me, you slammed a door in my face the other day."

If she thought to catch him off guard as she had that first day, she was disappointed. This time Jules was both unperturbed and prepared.

"Why this sudden drive to stir up old ghosts, Princess? Maybe it would be better just to let them be," he advised lightly.

"Why won't you tell me?" she persisted. "I know you know what happened. Is it because there's something shameful about it you want to hide?"

He looked down at her then for a long moment, as if reaching a decision. Slowly she saw the door close on her again. "The best of your life is ahead of you, Sabrina. Forget about the past," he said at last, his voice harsh and impersonal. "What happened back then is over and done with. It had nothing to do with you, so let it alone!"

Sabrina ducked down quickly to snap the leash she carried in her pocket on the golden retriever's collar, hiding tears of disappointment that welled up suddenly, unexpectedly in her eyes.

Her head still turned away, she said in a choked voice, "Well, I can't be friends on those terms. Come Hero." With a tug on the leash she set out blindly up the path.

At the crest of the embankment, she stole a furtive glance back over her shoulder toward the spot where a few moments ago he had kissed her. Jules stood where she had left him, his head turned to watch her go. Had she not steeled herself against the certain air of sadness she saw in his bearing, she would have obeyed her instinct to go back.

The new encounter with Jules Danner served only to make Sabrina more restless than she was before—so restless, in fact, that she found herself looking forward to Ralph Spurling's inevitable Friday call.

In his well-ordered life Ralph allowed himself one night a week for rest and recreation, "R & R" (Ralph's little joke). He set Saturday aside for physical fitness, followed by early-to-bed; and, since he made it a practice not to go out the night before any working day, that left Friday. All this he had explained on one of their early dates. He had called her every Friday for the past six months to ask her to have dinner with him that night.

Recently, Ralph had let Sabrina know obliquely that he was seriously interested in her and sometimes—like now—Sabrina could almost persuade herself that she might marry him someday when he reached the time for marriage in what he referred to as his "Master Plan." There was much to be said for Ralph. For one thing, he was not immature as were her college swains. He was dependable as well as good-looking and had a solid future ahead. She'd been told that his position in the insurance brokerage firm he worked for had "upward mobility," and that he owned a tidy amount of the company's stock. If she married him, there might be money, in time, to buy and restore Glenhaven.

But there her house of cards collapsed. Glenhaven how belonged to Jules Danner. The reminder of the exasperating, enigmatic son of her late father's partner for a moment drove all thought of Ralph Spurling from her mind. She moistened her lips dreamily, feeling again the hard, unexpected press of his mouth on hers; then shook the distraction angrily aside. Glenhaven did, indeed, belong to Jules Danner—not likely to ever be for sale again in her lifetime—and Jules Danner was not for her. Reluctantly she turned her thought back to the matter of Ralph Spurling and accepted the fact that if she decided to marry Ralph, she might as well quit listening for bells.

Bells or no bells, Sabrina was glad to be going out that night. In gratitude to Ralph for rescuing her from her doldrums for a time, she wore a new garnet red dress of silk *crepe de chine* that followed the lines of her body gently to the hips and then flared out in a dramatic froth of silk, giving her a wonderfully sensuous feeling as she moved. Great-grandmother Glendon's pearl and garnet necklace added the touch of elegance above the low neckline. The old-fashioned clasp seemed loose, and Sabrina worried whether or not it would hold. The deep red stones were so completely right with the dress that she couldn't resist wearing it but made a mental note to pay attention if she felt it slip.

She lifted the soft, ash-blond hair that hung almost to her shoulders and fastened the necklace carefully at the back of her neck. A fresh shampoo had added a touch of satin to her hair's normal sheen and brought out its natural wave. At the last minute she brushed a bit of color to her cheeks and a shadow of blue around the eyes to hid her unnatural paleness, that last telltale trace of a harrowing week.

Ralph had made dinner reservations, as usual, at the country club a few miles away where the dining room's Friday night specialty was lobster flown live from the Maine coast.

The place appeared more than usually busy tonight, and there was a short delay before the hostess was ready to seat them. While they waited for their table, other diners arrived. From where they stood near the reservations desk, Sabrina recognized a now all too familiar voice behind her.

"Really Jules, dining at the local country club is just *too* provincial. Couldn't you find a good restaurant? There must be some decent ones around." It was Rhonda Bartlett, petulant-voiced.

Over the deafening beat of her own erratic heart, Sabrina heard then the deep velvet baritone she expected—no, *waited for*—the voice that recently plagued her days and troubled her nights with dreams.

Jules Danner said, with a lazy laugh, "I'm sure there are, but this suits me very well. I like it, and the food is excellent. My dad still keeps the family membership, though he hasn't lived in Dutchess County for nearly twenty years."

In the next second he came into view, making his way to the reservations desk past where Sabrina stood with Ralph. She couldn't help noting that the man appeared as comfortably at home wearing a well-tailored glen plaid suit in subtly blended browns and a buff shirt and gold tie as he had in tattersall shirt and jeans. His eyes caught Sabrina. He paused and nodded a small, formal greeting.

"Ah, we meet again—luckily, on neutral ground," he said solemnly, but the glimmer in the dark blue eyes told her he was having a laugh at her expense. "I should hate to be thrown out before I ate my lobster." He dipped his head again and moved on as the dining room hostess arrived to show Sabrina and Ralph to their table.

"I didn't know you knew the great Jules Danner,"

Ralph said quizzically when they were seated with menus before them, and the hostess had gone on her way.

"Not really," Sabrina replied. She could only hope her face didn't look on fire, as certainly it felt to her. "I've run into him a couple of times. He was in the store the other day. How did you know who he was?"

"His picture was on the front page of the Poughkeepsie paper a couple of weeks ago with a two-column story. I thought everyone knew who he was."

"Two columns, front page—Poughkeepsie? What on earth for?"

"He's moved his company's headquarters there," Ralph said. "The man's gained a reputation as a wizard in electronics since he started his own company seven or eight years ago. He was known as an overnight boy-wonder a few years back. All the news magazines had interviews with him. You must have seen them at the time."

"At the age of fifteen I wasn't much interested in electronics geniuses and didn't read news magazines," Sabrina admitted laughingly. "I apparently have also overlooked his present splash in the Poughkeepsie paper. Do fill me in!"

"Just a lot of background stuff. He's bought one of the old—"

"He's bought my family's old home, Glenhaven," Sabrina interrupted impatiently. "I know that much. What else did the paper say?"

But it was clear Ralph felt the subject had received more attention already than it deserved. "That's about all," he said. "I didn't read it all that carefully."

Conversation lagged after that, insofar as Sabrina

was concerned. She managed to keep her ear tuned to Ralph's recital of insurance company affairs, murmuring appropriate "yes," "no," and "How interesting!" whenever called upon to give voice. Otherwise her thoughts shifted restlessly from one matter to another —the shop, Aunt Hat, the Great Wall of China; returning always to the newspaper article she had missed about Jules Danner.

When dinner was over, and they were on their way out, she couldn't have said whether she had eaten the lobster or the guinea hen. She knew somehow, intuitively, that Jules Danner at his table across the room had eyes on them as they went and was glad again for the garnet silk dress; grateful that Ralph, whatever his shortcomings, made such a presentable escort.

In the parking lot a few moments later as Ralph unlocked the car, Sabrina felt the clasp of the garnet necklace let go. Before she could stop it, the necklace had slithered down her body between the dress and her satin slip and dropped into fallen leaves at her feet. In the half-light of the parking lot she could see no sign of it until Ralph, always completely insured, came to the rescue with a pocket flashlight. The two of them huddled together sifting the bright leaves through their fingers.

"Ah, here we have it," said Ralph suddenly, holding the necklace out to her as he rose to his feet. From her own hunkered-down position, Sabrina's high-heeled sandals put her a bit off balance as she came up, throwing her into the arms of Ralph who steadied her until she stood solidly on her feet.

It was but an instant before he released her—just time enough for them to find themselves framed suddenly in the headlights of a departing car—a cream-colored Mercedes she'd seen before—from across the lot. The car passed nearby a moment later. Sabrina was dismayed to see Jules Danner viewing them with a saturnine eye through the window next to the driver's seat.

With a pale kiss from Ralph, they said good-night at her door on the stroke of eleven. Ralph said, "It's late now, Sabrina, but I've got something to discuss with you one of these evenings. Let's have an early dinner soon. I'll come up afterward and we can talk. I guess you know what about."

Somewhere inside, Sabrina's spirit yawned. Ralph was ready to propose marriage, and she wasn't ready to say *yes*. On the other hand, was she absolutely ready to give him a positive *no?* Thanks to Ralph's built-in time clock, she didn't have to come to grips with the question tonight.

Gently she pulled herself from his light embrace. "Good night Ralph," she said. She slipped through the door he had unlocked for her a moment before and into the house, securing the bolt when the door was closed. The golden retriever came bounding out of the kitchen and across the passageway to the foyer at the foot of the stairs in exuberant greeting.

Things had come to a pretty pass, she thought wistfully, when even the sight of her own dog was a sensuous reminder of the first moment Jules' mouth had taken possession of hers. She dropped to her knees and the rough red tongue licked her cheek in an ecstasy of affection.

"All right, Hero, that's enough, old dear," she said,

laughing as she pushed the dog away. "I must say, there's more to your kisses than there is to Ralph's."

She bedded the dog down with a final pat and went into the service porch where she opened a wooden bin in which she kept old newspapers, searching through those of the weeks past until she found the one she was looking for.

Upstairs in the living room she touched a match to the wood laid in the fireplace and closed the screen, leaving the fire to take hold while she went into her bedroom to change into night clothes.

Dressed for bed, Sabrina slipped on a robe of eiderdown the color of citron that Aunt Hat had given her the year she went away to college. In the easy comfort of the old robe, she headed for the living room, pausing in the little butler's pantry to brew a pot of orange-spice tea which she took with her to the blue-patterned wing chair before the fire.

She unfolded the newspaper and gazed for a long while at the ruggedly handsome face of Jules Danner that stared back at her with a touch of arrogance from the right-hand column of the paper's front page. At last she began to read and when she was finished, read again. She let the paper slip to the floor as she sipped her tea slowly and brooded into the flames.

The article about Jules made no more than a brief mention of the partnership between his father, Archibald Danner—"now of Manhattan," it said—and her own father, Harrison Burke; saying only that the partnership was dissolved a year before the business collapsed and Harrison Burke died.

Back to square one, thought Sabrina, ready to weep

from frustration. Not one smidgen of new information did the article contain about the partnership. The rest of it was about Jules. Still, she could hardly expect a newspaper to open doors her mother and aunt had arbitrarily closed on her eighteen years before and were clearly not to be opened by Jules.

She could understand and sympathize with her mother's silence, but why Jules's? Whatever happened had hurt her mother so deeply she henceforth shut all things related to it forever from her mind. Even the name of her dead husband brought such pain to the dear woman's eyes that out of love for her Sabrina and her aunt had kept it unspoken for as long as she was alive. In Sabrina's case, this meant not asking questions that might reopen the wound. It was a practice of such long standing that even after her mother's death until now, Sabrina had been reluctant to raise old ghosts.

The paper referred to Jules Danner as an "electronics genius" who had built his own company and made his first million before he was thirty-one. Now, four years later, he had moved his company's headquarters from the west coast to Poughkeepsie and had bought the old Glendon estate for his home.

"I spent my boyhood in this area," Danner was quoted as saying. "I often visited there as a youngster and thought it would be a fine place for a man to own."

So he had coveted Glenhaven all along!—"thought it would be a fine place to own"—Sabrina repeated to herself as she continued to read between the lines of the newspaper article, piecing together more of her family's tragedy than she had ever learned at home.

"Is it because there's something shameful you don't

want to tell?" she had asked him, not believing, just saying it in hopes it would make him talk; not even guessing that she had hit the nail squarely on the head.

For, of course, it *had* been something shameful. Why else would Jules close up like a clam and tell her to "leave it alone?" Something dishonorable had occurred, that much was clear. Her father must have caught Archibald Danner in some reprehensible business deal, and Jules was ashamed to tell her the truth.

The very fact the newspaper carefully avoided spelling out the circumstances surrounding the dissolution—fearing a libel suit, no doubt—made it easy enough to guess what had happened. It was not hard to see that Archibald Danner had somehow contrived to walk out with the partnership's assets on which he had grown comfortably rich; nor that Sabrina's father had been left with the firm's liabilities which had subsequently wiped him out. In a sense, Jules's father might be said to have been the cause of her own father's death, since the heart attack which killed him so short a time later was surely caused by the shock of his old partner's treachery and the collapse of his own world, she saw now.

No wonder Jules Danner had shut her out the moment she started to ask questions, counseled her to "Forget the past." Why, even today he was profiting from his father's ill-gotten gains. Where else had he gotten the money for his education and perhaps even for his own business start?

To think that after all this he could come back and brazenly set himself up as master of Glenhaven, the pride of Glendons and Burkes. Having administered such a posthumous *coup de grace* was it surprising he couldn't look Harrison Burke's daughter in the eyes?

Oh yes, the piecing together was easy, thought Sabrina bitterly and, in her bitterness, hated him. Hated Jules Danner, the most exciting, virile— *contemptible* man who would ever walk into her life.

Chapter Four

Leaving the shop to Ethel and Dora the following Monday morning, Sabrina drove upstate some thirty-five miles in her small Colt station wagon to look at an early colonial chest she had learned was for sale. Returning in the late afternoon, she felt reasonably lighthearted for the first time in a week as she took the exit off Route 9 for Sutton, satisfied that she had spent a useful and rewarding day. The chest had turned out to be a treasure, authentic colonial in splendid condition considering its age; and she had managed to banish every thought of Jules Danner as it occurred to her mind.

There was a fair amount of traffic on the old highway which ran parallel to the Hudson River for a distance, and she kept her eyes ahead despite the temptations of the flamboyant countryside at the peak of autumn color on either side of the road.

As she approached Glenhaven, two miles short of Sutton, she was alarmed when the third car in the oncoming line of traffic veered suddenly to the right. A second later cars traveling in both directions began to brake and swerve erratically. Moving up on the spot in her own vehicle, she gave a horrified gasp as a streak of golden red flashed past the front wheels of the auto ahead of her, down a slight embankment at the right and up against the fieldstone wall that separated the grounds of Glenhaven from the old highway. As it came to a stop the streak took the shape of a broad-skulled dog with a plumey tail.

It was Hero! Either the trashman let him out, or he'd found a new escape on his own.

As if he hadn't just come within inches of being killed, the animal righted himself and bounded on with careless unconcern, following the ivy-covered wall to the driveway which he entered as if he belonged.

Jaw set with determination, Sabrina turned the little maroon station wagon sharply into the driveway in time to see Hero gambol across the lawn toward the fieldstone house with its curved wooden portico.

She applied her brakes and steered off to the side. Stepping from the car onto the blacktop drive, she was about to shout for the dog but remembered the open gate that suggested someone else on the premises and toned down her voice.

"Hero!" she called sharply, softly, not wishing to reach Jules Danner's ears should he be somewhere around. She was relieved to see the red dog come to a stop and turn to look back at her curiously. He flourished the feathery tail in recognition but made no move to come rushing to greet her. She edged toward him cautiously, cooing endearments as she came.

"Come Hero—good dog—nice dog. Come here," she wheedled gently. "Come on, old friend. It's time to go home." Still the dog didn't budge but watched her come until she was only a few feet away. Then, with a rumble of delight, the animal turned and frolicked off, stopping at intervals to look back and make sure she was still in the game.

As she drew near the house in hot pursuit she became ever more concerned that she might run into Jules Danner. For a moment she considered giving in to an urge to flee and letting the fool dog get home as best he could, but the memory of the crazy red streak shooting heedlessly in front of the wheels of the moving car renewed her purpose.

"Darn you Hero, come back!" she panted futilely as the creature disappeared around the corner of the house.

Across the lazy slope of the land she ran through ankle-high grass and weeds that had felt no mower in a long time. She was hardly dressed for this, she thought angrily as one high heel of her favorite saddle-leather pumps hit some hidden obstacle and came up with a long, ugly scratch. They were not made for running, but at least her jade green skirt was cut with a flare and the matching belted sweater was knit with a soft full sleeve and open-necked collar that gave her some room to breathe.

Even so, she found herself panting as she neared the great fieldstone house and followed the path the errant dog had traveled as he took himself out of her sight. In a last blind burst of speed she rounded the corner and came up smack against a human obstacle.

The force of the collision sent her reeling, and she closed her eyes as two strong, sinewy arms caught her and pulled her close against the warm bulwark of a tall, muscular man.

Half-dazed and breathing heavily, Sabrina hadn't the strength or desire to pull herself free. For a moment she let herself rest there, her cheek caressed by the soft cashmere sweater he wore. Beneath it she heard the swift, sure beat of his heart.

As her breathing grew normal, a breathlessness of another sort took hold. A new, warm, never-before discovered wellspring of excitement gushed up from the very center of her being. The rush of her beating heart was now caused not by her recent run, but by something mysterious inside her that rose and surged and sang and caused her, without willing it, to cling to the man and press herself closer to him while her body savored a gusty joy. She felt his face settle gently on the top of her head, his breath whispering through her hair like a truant breeze.

"Ah, little Princess, welcome home," said Jules Danner, somewhere above her head. The moment shattered into a million fragments like a bauble on a Christmas tree.

"Let me go!" Sabrina gasped, struggling to pull herself free. As in her dreams the arms held her tightly, refusing to release her. She looked over Jules Danner's elbow at the golden retriever standing nearby watching the proceedings. The dog moved restlessly as if to serve notice he was about to take off on another round of his game.

"Stay!" said Jules Danner quietly, and Hero stayed; then "Sit!" and the red dog sat.

Traitor! said Sabrina silently, furious with the beast as she redoubled her efforts to escape. But no physical act of hers would free her from this man until he was quite ready to let her go. She gave up after a moment, feeling the struggle was demeaning.

Summoning all of her dignity, she said coldly, "Will you please let me go?"

"What's your hurry, Princess," he said reasonably, as to a difficult child. "You've been in my arms before, you know—and on these very same grounds."

The arrogance of the man! Would he never let her forget he had rescued her? She wouldn't give him the satisfaction of an acknowledgment. "I don't know what you are talking about," she said distantly.

"Of course you don't, little Sabrina Glendon Burke. You don't remember. I was twelve years old, and you must have been about two," Jules Danner said in an amused voice. She saw the flicker of a muscle in his cheek; then saw no more as his face came down, and his seeking mouth found hers. Time and her heart stood still. Almost reluctantly, it seemed, he loosened his hold on her.

"I kissed you, little Princess," he repeated softly, "but it was never such a kiss as that."

Still clasping her arms, he held her away from him and surveyed her coolly from head to toe. Under the searching gaze Sabrina felt the color rise in her face. She was suddenly painfully aware of the ridiculous figure she cut in her ruined shoes, her hair blowing wildly and her skirt askew.

The man nodded his head, as if in approval; at the same time Sabrina saw a sardonic glint in his eyes.

"The pretty baby grew up to be a beautiful young lady—and a frisky one, if one is to judge by the way she nuzzles her escorts in parking lots," he said with a short laugh.

"Nuzzles!" she exploded. "I was not nuzzling. I'll have you know I dropped—," she broke off with a gasp of fury. She wasn't going to win this round either. She didn't owe the man an explanation anyhow. She didn't owe Jules Danner anything.

"Come, Hero. Let's go," she said coldly.

She turned on her heel and walked away but was obliged to go back when the dog declined to pick up the cue. She was acutely aware of the half-smile on the face of the man as she returned. Pretending he wasn't there, she exercised all her wiles and cunning to lure the dog from where the man had told him to sit. Short of grabbing the big animal by the neck and dragging him across an acre of weedy grass, which was quite beyond her power, she could see no way to get the beast back to the car. Tears of frustration were close to her eyes.

The impasse was broken at length by a low whistle from Danner which brought the dog to his feet and at the man's side in a bound.

"Looks like I'll have to get this rascal out to your car," Jules Danner said smugly.

"Kindly don't trouble yourself," snapped Sabrina. "The last thing I need is help from you."

The man gave a chiding cluck. "Aha, Sabrina, we're going to have to do something about that temper of yours," he said with a wicked grin. "You look very pretty when you are mad, but I'm glad we're on my

68

ground. I have a feeling you might throw me out if we happened to be on yours."

"I don't need your gratuitous reminder that Glenhaven belongs to you," said Sabrina frostily. "You may rest assured I would ask you to leave if it still belonged to the Burkes."

To her humiliation, the red-gold dog dealt her into the hands of her enemy by the simple expedient of settling down on his haunches and refusing to move for her. She couldn't just walk away and leave him there, though she was sorely tempted. There was no way out of it but to let Jules Danner take charge.

With no further talk between them, the man bent down and hoisted the big animal up on one shoulder and draped him around his neck. Wearing the creature like a fur piece, with the plume of tail waving cheerfully off to one side, he went the way she had come, across the sloping grounds to the driveway and her station wagon, with a jaunty stride. Sabrina followed, feeling thoroughly depressed and at the same time more than a little bemused.

By all rights she should despise Jules Danner, yet something inside her cried out to hold on to that one lovely moment in the shelter of his arms. In her heart she could not reject the stunning rapture she had never before known or completely understood.

When she arrived at the car, Hero had been stowed in the back from which there was no escape, and Jules Danner in his dark red cashmere sweater and gray flannel slacks was striding purposefully away from her toward the house. Sabrina slammed the door sharply when she got in behind the wheel, but the man did not turn at the sound to look back. She made a U-turn in the driveway and headed out, bewildered by the muddied feelings that roiled deep inside.

By the time she turned into the highway, Hero had lumbered over the back of the seat beside her and settled his head in her lap with such a look of dumb contrition she took her hand off the wheel and gave the dog a forgiving scratch behind the ears.

"All right, you wicked dog. You're forgiven, but it was all your fault. Don't let it happen again," she said ruefully; but she could not so lightly dismiss the contradictions in her heart. She tried, with a kind of desperation, to sort out and understand the ambivalent passions the mere thought of Jules Danner aroused in her. Neither he nor his father, who had presided over her own father's downfall, deserved anything but hostility from the daughter of Harrison Burke.

Why then, as she watched the tall, broad-shouldered man turn without a word that afternoon and lope away from her with the cool, splendid grace of some jungle beast, had she somehow felt bereaved? How explain the sudden rapture that flamed in her heart at the unexpected sound of his voice and the traitorous wish that Ralph Spurling were such a man?

Even as she struggled to understand these contradictions and made an inward vow to stay clear of the man, she discovered in herself a burning desire to see the inside of Glenhaven one last time, even at the risk of running into him again.

The only clear picture she carried with her of the splendid interior of the old Tudor mansion was of resting her small chin on the writing board of the tambour desk in an upstairs bay window that overlooked the Hudson, as she watched her mother's pen make strange squiggles on ivory notepaper with violet ink.

Of the other rooms—their rich furnishings and ornamentation, their dimensions and locations in relation to each other—she could never be sure whether the pictures in her mind came from actual memory or whether they were wistful images fashioned from what she'd been told. Was there really a broad, winding staircase up from the reception hall under a dome of colored glass? Unless she slipped back now before Jules Danner moved into the house, she would never know.

She made a plan that was simple and direct, based on a likelihood that during business hours Jules Danner did whatever he had to do at his company headquarters in Poughkeepsie. Her hindsight told her that the unfortunate Monday meeting might never have occurred had the hour been closer to three than to five.

Next time she would go in the early afternoon and park the station wagon inconspicuously outside the gate from where she could steal up the driveway to a point where she could see if his car was by the carriage house or in the circular drive. How she was actually to get inside the house was another matter. It was hardly likely it could even be done. Her best hope was for chinks of some kind where she could at least get a peek at some of the downstairs rooms.

So it was, on Thursday in the early afternoon, Sabrina left the shop in the hands of Ethel and Dora once more and took the highway out of Sutton the short distance to Glenhaven. There she parked the Colt in the shadow of the fieldstone fence and slipped through the open gate.

Within sight of the parking areas she drew a quick

breath of relief. No cream-colored Mercedes! Instead there was a green pickup truck with a ladder in back and a logo on the door that read Fanner & Sons, general contractors. Beyond the weathered portico the massive double doors had been propped wide open. She could scarcely believe her luck.

Approaching, Sabrina could look all the way through the doors to the large empty reception hall and see the bottom of the curved stairway whose broad steps fanned out in a graceful sweep to the hall.

Standing back from the house, she hesitated a moment before she ventured on, her eyes following the graceful front line of the fieldstone, unblemished by time or neglect. In spite of its appearance of solidarity the old mansion reminded her, somehow, of an aging *grande dame* who has fallen on hard times. In a way she should be grateful to Jules Danner for whatever cosmetic aid he might give to the dear old place. With a face-lift and that indestructible body, she could be as good as new.

The reception hall extended upward past the second story to a shallow dome-shaped skylight of Tiffany glass. Through it the autumn sun streamed down to cast light patterns on the inlaid hardwood floor. Sabrina caught her breath in sudden memory of the little girl who had been herself, chasing light patterns across that same parquet floor a long time ago.

Except for two wooden planks supported by a pair of sawhorses, the great hall was bare. Sabrina was about to climb the steps and look down from the circular balcony as she now remembered she had done as a child, when she heard voices from a room above. Having no wish to run into the contractor or his men, she stepped back under the balcony's overhang where she could not be seen from above.

As she hesitated there, her attention was caught by a large roll of blueprints on the makeshift table formed by the sawhorses and boards. She couldn't resist rolling the papers out to take a look at what Jules Danner was thinking to do with the house.

The prints included floor plans and elevations and the name of Hadley Fields, a New York architect, famous enough to be somewhat familiar to her. At first glance Sabrina could make no sense out of the drawings. Thinking them plans for some other project, she was about to roll them up again, disappointed, when something about them caused her to look again and see them for what they were—completed blueprints for converting the Tudor style manor-house into a modern glass and stone structure designed to sever all ties with the past. When the work was done, Jules Danner would have successfully erased from the house all traces of Glendons and Burkes.

In her shock, Sabrina was quite unaware she was no longer alone until voices behind her brought her around to find Rhonda Bartlett standing by the stairway in the company of a stout gray-bearded man. Sabrina was too stunned by what she had just seen to make an effort to explain her own presence in the house.

"What is Jules Danner doing to Glenhaven?" she demanded in a choked voice.

"Well, if it isn't the little antique dealer," said the decorator in a nasty tone. "What are you doing, hiding back there in the shadows?"

"He can't be serious—these ridiculous plans—,"

Sabrina cried, her voice trembling with sorrow and disbelief as she held up the telltale prints.

"My dear Ms. Burke," Ms. Bartlett said impatiently, "I happen to be the decorator, and this is the architect. We are here to meet with the contractor. Just what are you doing here?"

Sabrina was close to tears. "He's done away with the bay window," she said dully. "There's not even a *place* for the tambour desk."

"Desk? Oh, that's not for here. The desk is for an old brownstone I'm decorating. It looks out over the East River in Manhattan," said the decorator. "We've never had any intention of using antiques here."

"But *why?*" asked Sabrina in a stunned voice.

This time it was the architect who spoke. "My dear young woman, my plans are too dramatic, too contemporary to be furnished with antiques. Mr. Danner wants light, so I've designed a tremendous cantilevered deck to run the full width of the house and overhang a complete wall of glass on the west side overlooking the Hudson. We'll use the existing fieldstone from walls we will tear down," he explained loftily.

"It's a divine plan," the decorator said, leaving Sabrina no room to speak. "Everything will be light and bright, the way Jules wants it, off-white with startling splashes of color to bring it alive. Does that sound like *antiques?*"

"It will look like a cocktail lounge," protested Sabrina.

"But that's really no concern of yours, now is it, Ms. Burke?" asked Ms. Bartlett. Her deliberately patronizing tone fanned the flame of Sabrina's indignation.

"It most certainly is," she cried. "My mother's

ancestors built Glenhaven. It was my family's home for generations until about twenty years ago."

"Oh yes. I believe Jules did mention something about that," said the decorator indifferently. "Well, no matter. We have work to do. That's the contractor and his man rattling around upstairs. Come, Hadley." The decorator turned her back on Sabrina and led the way upstairs.

With little heart for any further survey of Glenhaven, Sabrina did not stay. She lingered only a moment for a last sad upward look at the Tiffany skylight which the architect's plans would tear out and took leave of her old home, knowing it was unlikely she would ever step in it again.

As she walked slowly down the steps, the cream-colored Mercedes turned into the driveway, and a moment later Jules Danner pulled into the parking circle and stepped out of the car. Sabrina's first instinct was to flee, but she had second thoughts. Summoning all her courage, she squared her shoulders and set out across the grounds, a small, pretty young woman in a red blazer and navy blue pleated skirt, marching forth to face the enemy, her spirit quailing inside.

"Ah, Princess," Jules Danner called out as he walked forward in his inimitable long-limbed stride to meet her. "To what do I owe this unexpected visit?" There was a quizzical half-smile on his face and a waiting look in the deep-set eyes.

Face flushed, heart beating swiftly as after a long run, Sabrina wasted no time on civilities but came straight to the point.

"You don't seriously intend to put Glenhaven in the hands of those two house-wreckers, I hope!" she cried, struggling to keep the quaver from her voice and at the same time fix him directly with her eye.

The handsome brows arched in surprise. "I have no idea what you are talking about," he said.

"Oh, I think you do," Sabrina retorted hotly. "I really think you do. I'm talking about that self-inflated architect in there from Manhattan and your great and good friend, the decorator."

The good humor disappeared from his eyes, leaving them wintry. The line of his mouth set imperiously. She realized that she was making a mess of it. If only the man wouldn't treat her like a silly schoolgirl, she thought crossly, maybe she wouldn't fall apart in his presence whenever they met. She hadn't said a word she wanted to, and what she had said had come out all wrong.

"My dear Sabrina," said Jules Danner coldly, "Hadley Fields is a highly respected architect in New York City and while you may not like Ms. Bartlett's personality, her reputation as a decorator is above reproach. Whatever expertise you may feel you have in such matters would hardly be a match for theirs."

In the sudden change of mood Sabrina saw her time running out, and she'd still made no plea for the house. The stern, unyielding face filled her with a yearning despair as she tried again for words to persuade Jules Danner that he must call a halt to havoc—the blueprints for which she had just seen.

"I have no doubt Mr. Fields and Ms. Bartlett are highly respected in the metropolitan world," she conceded stiffly and, considering her state of mind, with as much tact as she could bring to bear, "but is their thinking right for Glenhaven? Shouldn't you look for someone with a sense of history and a more traditional point of view?"

The man's face suddenly wore a mask of angered pride. The haughty look that came into his eyes told Sabrina unmistakably that Jules Danner was not accustomed to being told how to run his affairs. Could this be the same man who had caught her up in his arms a few short days before? Her heart cried out to the Jules Danner who had held her then. For an instant, as if it would bring him back, she closed her eyes. When she opened them again, she saw nothing to lend comfort to her flagging spirit.

"Serving the interest of Glenhaven's history is no longer up to you, Sabrina," he said, sarcasm lending a cutting edge to the deep baritone voice. "It so happens I'm not entirely satisfied with Glenhaven as it stands. For instance, the drawing room has always been dark. It needs to be opened out to bring in more light and take advantage of the view. Since those things are out of my line I've hired professionals who know what they are doing to apply their talents to what I have in mind. You may rest assured, I consider them quite capable of working within the context of Glenhaven's glorious past. I suggest you stay out of their hair."

Sabrina's face flamed with humiliation, then her whole being blazed in a fire of anger that burned away whatever sentimentality there remained in her heart. How could she forget the enemy was Jules Danner when he made such a point of showing her he was?

"Are you telling me to leave?" she asked, the sarcasm in her voice a match for his.

"Well, one might say it's my turn," he said wryly.

Reaching out, he cupped her chin in one hand and tipped her face up to meet his, stilling her acid answer with a kiss. Against her struggle he did not release her but continued to hold her face and study it with brooding eyes.

He was the enemy! She knew she must tear herself free, but she had no will to move.

After a moment he suddenly took his hand away from her chin and with a tender, relentless pressure, cradled her head on his arm. The strong, sensuous mouth came down upon hers, even as she resisted, with such a devastating force she clung to the man. Her own traitorous lips softened under the demanding press of his, parting in a sort of welcoming surrender to the gentle flick of his tongue as streaks of fire shot, like bright arrows, through her body.

For time without measure he held her thus. Then softly, deliberately he withdrew and set her free. With a steadying hand on her shoulder, his unfathomable eyes watched her in that same brooding way until she put the moment of dreams behind her and stood solidly on her feet. After a time she breathed a trembling sigh and looked up at him, far too shaken to speak.

To her dismay, Jules Danner took his hand from her shoulder and without so much as a gesture or word of farewell he turned and headed across the grounds to the house. As he went, he began to whistle a haunting, free-form tune that stirred in Sabrina such a sense of bewildered loneliness that she watched the departing figure through a blur of tears.

Watching, her bewilderment turned to hurt and the

hurt to anger and guilt. By the time he disappeared into the house her last remaining emotion was a furious self-contempt.

She started down the driveway to her car outside the gate in a fast run, as if in running it were possible to escape her dreams.

Chapter Five

That night Sabrina dreamed again of Jules Danner, an improbable dream in which she saw him striding masterfully into the store to sweep her into his arms, the velvet baritone murmuring in her ear, "Have no fear, dear Sabrina. For your sake, Glenhaven will be spared."

Restlessly she prowled the shop next day, swirling a dustcloth over bric-a-brac, winding the clocks, rearranging displays; reminding herself derisively that even if such an unlikely happening could occur there was no future in it—not for the son of Archibald Danner and the daughter of Harrison Burke.

Haunted by thoughts of Jules Danner and the fate of Glenhaven, she quite overlooked that the day was Friday. She accepted Ralph's invitation to dinner perfunctorily when he called and scarcely noticed he was a half hour late in picking her up, though she had never known it to happen before.

She listened with detachment to Ralph's tale of woe having to do with a flat tire and a long wait for a repairman to fix it. It was plain to see he was out of sorts, a condition he demonstrated shortly when he learned the dining room hostess at the crowded country club had let their table go when they failed to appear, venting his ill humor by unreasonably ordering her to conjure up a table for them *now!* Otherwise, he would take the matter to the manager.

Before the impending scene could develop, a familiar voice said over Ralph's shoulder to the hostess, "They may share my table, if they care to."

Sabrina's heart gave a startled leap and, in spite of herself, she turned her head, as did her escort. There was Jules Danner standing but a few feet behind them. In his imposing presence, Ralph suddenly appeared dwarfed. Jules held out a hand.

"I'm Jules Danner," he said to Ralph. "I don't believe we've met. Sabrina and I are old friends. I just found out the two people who were to have dinner with me were unavoidably detained in the city, so I have a table for three. You're welcome to join me." There was a taunting glint in the eyes that turned on her briefly and then away.

In response to her light but well-aimed kick, Ralph looked around at her reproachfully but ignored the slight negative shake of her head and the silent *"No!"* she mouthed.

"I'm Ralph Spurling," he said. "If it wouldn't be putting you out—"

"Not at all. If you'll excuse me, I'll take care of it with the hostess," said Jules. He stepped around them to the small desk where the hostess had gone on to other patrons, leaving Sabrina and her escort momentarily to themselves.

Sabrina fairly hissed at Ralph, "Come on. Let's get out of here. I'm not going to share any table with him!"

"Why not?" asked Ralph but didn't wait for an answer. "We'll never find a decent place to eat without reservations at this hour. Besides, I've been looking for a chance to meet Danner. Between his company's employees and his real property and everything else he owns, do you realize how much insurance that guy must be buying every year?"

There wasn't a moment for Sabrina to say more. Short of making a scene herself, there was nothing to do but go along as the hostess led them to a table; though she felt like a captive of the two men at her heels and betrayed by both—Ralph, who was willing to sell her out at the mere thought of an insurance bonanza and Jules for offering the table just to have the fun of watching her squirm.

She had not yet spoken to Jules. Now, as he stepped in front of Ralph to pull out a chair for her, she was determined not to give him the satisfaction of seeing she was upset. She looked at him from under a curve of long lashes and gave him her most dazzling smile.

"Thank you so much. This is very kind of you," she murmured; then, in a biting parody of Rhonda Bartlett, "Ralph does so hate to wait, don't you darling?" She turned a sweet smile on Ralph who blinked in surprise. She was somewhat piqued when Jules again stepped easily around Ralph and took the seat across the table

82

from her, leaving the one by her side to Ralph. After a moment she became aware that from across the table Jules could study her with those dark, enigmatic eyes. She glanced down at the menu self-consciously, painfully conscious that a new flush of color had rushed to her cheeks.

For a moment she was unreasonably glad she had changed her mind about wearing the blue-gray Qiana that matched her mood. At the last minute, almost absently, she had slipped into her favorite dress, a plum-colored wool that brought out the violet blue of her eyes and was cut with a deep V neckline. She and her aunt had seen it one day in a Lord & Taylor window on Fifth Avenue and she had resolutely turned away; but when her birthday rolled around a few weeks later she found it waiting for her on the table in a chic box.

If she had worn the more becoming dress as a gracious gesture to Ralph, the effort was lost. Hardly were the menus whisked away when he turned his attention to the man across the table as if he had forgotten Sabrina was there. How many employees did Danner have on his payroll? How large was his physical plant?—business questions Danner answered politely, laconically, before directing the conversation to include her. Even then, Sabrina found Ralph managed to edge her out.

"Is your red-haired friend under lock and key tonight?" Jules asked at one point, darting her a wicked glance. Before she could answer, Ralph picked it up.

"Oh, you mean the dog? I'm not much on dogs, myself; and that one's nothing but a nuisance. I keep telling her to get rid of the no-good mutt," he confided in a kind of good-buddy voice to Jules.

The two dark wings that were Jules's eyebrows shot up. "You don't say!" He turned to Sabrina. "If you ever decide to take Spurling's advice, I'd like to have Hero on whatever terms you may ask."

"So you know Hero!" Ralph broke in heartily, as if he saw a need to curry favor.

"I've seen him at Glenhaven a time or two," Danner replied curtly.

"Oh, yes, Glenhaven!" Spurling picked it up with spurious enthusiasm. "That's a beautiful old mansion you bought yourself, Jules. Sabrina's old family home, you know. I've been told it's one of the oldest on the river, a real historical monument. I hope you have it insured for everything it's worth."

Danner eyed him coolly for a moment before he said, with a short laugh, "You're an insurance salesman, I presume."

"Broker, not *salesman*," Spurling hastened to correct him and named his company. "Fastest growing insurance brokerage corporation outside of Manhattan. Since you brought it up, Jules, I'd like to go over your insurance program one of these days with you."

Jules gave him a cold look and turned to Sabrina. "Speaking of Glenhaven," he said, "you might be interested to know that the two who were to have dinner with me tonight are Rhonda Bartlett and Hadley Fields. You may as well know—"

But Sabrina had held her peace as long as she could. "I am not interested in your conspiracy to destroy Glenhaven. Kindly spare me the details of your dealings with that pair." She saw the muscles in Jules's face grow taut, a sudden hauteur in his eyes.

"As you wish," he said distantly.

"Now Sabrina, don't be too hasty!" Ralph cautioned, jumping into the breach. "You *could* be mighty interested in Glenhaven if Jules, here, decided to insure the place with me. Now isn't that right?" he added with a meaningful smirk.

Sabrina pushed back her chair and stood up. "You'll have to excuse me," she said to Ralph wearily, ignoring Jules who had politely risen, too. "Would you mind asking for the check? I'd like to get home. I feel a headache coming on."

"But we haven't had dessert."

"I'll wait for you in the lobby." She left them, the piercing fury of Danner's eyes, as he watched her go, burning like hot coals upon her back.

On the way home a short time later, Ralph said querulously, "I don't know what got into you tonight, Sabrina. I've never seen you act like this."

She blinked guiltily and herded her attention away from her own cheerless brooding to focus on her escort. "I'm sorry," she apologized. On impulse she confided, "It's all because of Glenhaven. I'm sick about what Jules Danner's going to do to the place."

"Since when is Danner confiding in you?" Ralph asked suspiciously.

"He isn't, of course!" Sabrina's voice was impatient. "I just happened to see the blueprints, and they're awful. I can't let him get away with it. I've got to stop him somehow."

"Don't be silly. You can't. The property is his," said Ralph with disdain. "Let's don't waste the rest of the evening on your lost cause."

As Sabrina fished through her purse for the key to

her door a few minutes later, Ralph reminded her that he was expecting to be asked in. "There's something it's about time we start talking about, Sabrina. I thought we had agreed that tonight . . ." Reproachfully, he left it unfinished. "I guess you know—"

She stopped him there. "Oh, Ralph, I can't think of anything I care to discuss with you now," she said pointedly.

As if to sidestep the implications, Spurling hastened to withdraw. "I know. I know. You've got a headache. It's all because of Danner and that old house. I suppose it'd better wait for another night." He held out his hand for the key. "Here. I'll unlock the door."

"Never mind," said Sabrina shortly. "I'll do it." Before he could lay a hand on her to administer the customary pallid kiss, she stepped inside. "Thanks for dinner, Ralph. Good-night."

She stood in the entry hall and looked up the stairs to the light she had left on in the empty living room, suddenly awash in a sea of loneliness. With something akin to panic she wondered for a moment if Ralph had taken their scene at the door as the dismissal she had intended it for. Maybe she should think about it some more. He didn't ring bells. On the other hand, he was all she had.

"*. . . beautiful old mansion you bought yourself, Jules . . . oldest on the river . . . real historical monument . . .*"

Ironically, these words, spoken by Ralph at that unfortunate dinner and remembered by Sabrina as she got ready for bed that night were the clue to her means of keeping Jules Danner from proceeding with the plans to contemporize Glenhaven. For Glenhaven was, indeed, a historical monument. Hadn't General George Washington, himself, visited her Glendon ancestors there, during the Revolutionary Army's West Point campaign? How Sabrina wished now that she had the power to do as the Vanderbilts and the Roosevelts had done and deed Glenhaven to the government. Still, there must be some way the public could preserve the historical past against the wanton destruction of private landowners. Uncle George Channing would know.

George Channing had been the Glendon family attorney for three generations and a close friend of Sabrina's grandfather. A frequent guest at Glenhaven during her Grandfather Glendon's days, he had been given the honorary title of "uncle" by Sabrina's mother when she was a little girl. It was a title Sabrina carried on with affection.

If Uncle George couldn't come up with a way to protect her particular historical monument, then it simply couldn't be done.

Though in his late eighties now, the old gentleman was blessed with a shrewd and able mind that never flickered. When Sabrina burst in upon him that morning, he had just snipped off the end of the first of four cigars he would allow himself that day and was sniffing and fondling it gently before putting it to the flame.

"Ah, Sabrina, dear child, how good to see you, my dear," he said. With a fleeting look of regret, he tucked the unlighted cigar carefully into a breast pocket and rose with courtly dignity to embrace the breathless young woman and give her a fatherly kiss.

"You're getting to look more like your beautiful mother every day of your life."

"Thank you, Uncle George. You're looking wonderful, too," said Sabrina, much too fond of the aging gentleman to do him the discourtesy of rushing amenities. His fingers played wistfully with the cigar in his pocket.

"Go on, Uncle George. Smoke it. I don't mind," Sabrina urged. He allowed himself to be persuaded.

"Now, dear child, what brings you here?" he asked when the cigar was burning well and all courtesies had been observed.

"Jules Danner is going to ruin Glenhaven," she said, getting to the point at once. "You've got to find a way to stop him, Uncle George."

"Come, come child," the old lawyer soothed. "It can't be that bad. Jules is a good boy. Besides that, he's smart. He's not going to do anything that will harm Glenhaven."

"I beg your pardon, Uncle George. You haven't seen what he's up to. He's going to destroy that beautiful old house," Sabrina cried.

"How's he going to do that, Sabrina?"

"He's hired this Manhattan architect, a sort of latter-day Frank Lloyd Wright, and they're going to put an all-glass wall on the side facing the Hudson. As if that weren't enough, they're going to use the fieldstone they tear out to build a monstrous cantilevered overhang above it."

Uncle George Channing pondered this for a moment, his shrewd old eyes studying Sabrina from across the desk.

"You sure about this, Sabrina?"

"Of course I'm sure. The architect told me himself. You don't think I'd bother you if I didn't know it to be a fact?" Sabrina said defensively. "Isn't there something the law can do?"

The old man took off his glasses. Leaning back in his big reclining chair he closed his eyes. The old darling must be close to ninety, Sabrina thought as she swallowed her impatience. His eyes opened as she was beginning to wonder if he'd fallen asleep. They were bright and alert.

"I've been thinking about Jules, Sabrina," the old man said. "I know his father. I knew Jules as a child, like I know your dear mother and you. The point is this: What you're telling me, honey, just doesn't sound like any Danner I ever knew."

"How do you mean?"

Squinting like a wise old owl, George Channing told her, "Well, in the first place, that family's always had a fine feeling for the past. The kind of jazzed-up place you describe is not their style. What's more to the point, if he wanted a contemporary showplace, Jules wouldn't have bought Glenhaven. He would build himself one."

"That doesn't change the fact that he did buy Glenhaven, and I've seen the blueprints for what he plans to do with it," she insisted stubbornly. "Please! Can't you do something to stop him, Uncle George?"

"My dear child, you've said yourself the place belongs to Jules. He can festoon it with gargoyles or paint all the rooms black, if he likes."

"You mean I can't stop him?"

"Well, you don't have any claim on the place, Sabrina," the lawyer reminded her. "If I were you, I wouldn't worry about it. Trust Jules. He's not going to hurt Glenhaven."

"Could we have it declared a historical landmark?"

The old man nodded. "Yes, well, that would make a difference, all right. Once the landmark people agree to so designate it, whatever is done subsequently must be in keeping with the building's original intent and approved in advance by them."

Sabrina brightened visibly. "Well, then, that's the answer. How do you go about getting it done?"

"Now Sabrina, are you sure you want to go through with this?" the lawyer asked mildly. "If Jules is ready to go on with this building, this could cause him not only a delay but a peck of trouble and expense. He's not going to like it at all."

It was plain the old fellow was dragging his feet. "It's going to take some time," he told her. "The wheels of the gods grind slowly."

Sabrina eyed him affectionately for a moment. Then she sighed and got to her feet. "Oh, all right, Uncle George," she said gently. "Don't worry about it. If you don't want to do it, I'll get someone else."

George Channing puffed his cigar for a moment. Finally, impatiently, he said, "Sit down. Sit down. If you're bound and determined, it better be me, I guess. I'll petition the landmark people to get things rolling."

"There's not a lot of time," she reminded him anxiously. "The contractor was out there last week. Is there any way to stop things right now?"

Again Channing puffed his cigar. "All right, Sabrina," he said reluctantly at last. "I can get out a restraining order, I suppose. That'll stop activity on the place until the landmark issue is cleared."

Leaving, Sabrina dropped a kiss in the middle of the old gentleman's bald pate. She knew she should feel elated at having engineered a reprieve, however tenuous, for Glenhaven; but she did not. Uncle George's reluctance to join in the effort made her somehow feel small. His words as she left stayed in her mind.

"Jules is not going to sit still for this, Sabrina," he warned. "Mark my word, you'll hear from him."

By afternoon of the third day following her visit to the old attorney, Sabrina could think of nothing but the predicted confrontation with Jules. Every time the silver bells on the shop door jingled, her heart set up a kind of frantic syncopation. She couldn't be sure whether her skittishness was due to apprehension over the stormy scene she knew lay ahead or the thought of being in the man's disturbing presence again, a prospect—though she was ashamed to admit it, even to herself—that seemed somehow worth all the unpleasantness it involved.

By midafternoon, when business had slacked off, Ethel stuck her head around the screen where Sabrina was working and asked if she could take the rest of the day off. Sabrina gladly let her go. It was no trick to leave her account books from time to time to take care of the occasional customer, and she welcomed the break it gave her from columns of figures plagued by the distractions of impossible dreams.

For since the morning when Jules hand first touched her shoulder she had built a library of precious moments that lay always in wait to seduce her thoughts—moments sternly banished only to steal into her mind again. In idle fantasy she found herself reliving each time they had touched: first, hand to her shoulder; then his arms enfolding her trembling body after the rescue

91

in the woods. Her senses called back the beat of his heart beneath her cheek, the heat that radiated from his body through hers as he cradled her close and carried her up out of the darkness into the light.

She knew each kiss by heart, from the first light, almost experimental brush of his lips on hers to the last passionate seeking—the acid taste of anger still in their mouths. With bitterness she reviewed them now.

As the day grew late, and she worked her way down through a spindle stacked with bills, she at last gave up looking for Danner. It was evident he would rather suffer a delay to his plans than endure the unpleasantness of another meeting with her. Deep down inside, the small worm of disappointment gnawed at Sabrina. She would never have believed Jules Danner would let his plans be thwarted without so much as lifting a hand.

The figures blurred before her eyes and disappeared. Her teeth played absently with the cap of the pen in her hand. She felt she had been betrayed.

Not that it would do him any good to storm into the store and blow off his annoyance at her; not even if his anger cooled, and—with that unmatched arrogance she'd seen before—he seized her in his arms and tried to win her with kisses. No, not even then would she agree to let him dismantle Glenhaven. She would tear herself from his embrace. She would . . .

The sudden, unexpected jingle of silver bells on the front door snapped her out of her reverie and to her feet in a startled leap that sent books and papers flying in all directions. *What is the matter with you, Sabrina Burke?* she asked herself.

Then from the front of the store the angry baritone

voice she had been awaiting three days boomed across the length of the shop to her alcove.

"Hello! Is there anyone here?" the voice of Jules Danner thundered through the small shop. Sabrina was filled with a senseless panic. Stumbling over fallen books and papers, she skirted the little tambour desk in one quick movement and made a mindless dash for the door that opened into the hallway to the living part of the house. Jules Danner was at her heels.

"Oh, no you don't, Sabrina Burke," he said almost in her ear, his voice grim. "Don't think you can run away."

She was through the door, but he was right behind her. Three steps into her private domain, she was brought to an abrupt halt by strong hands that pinned her against the stairway wall. The eyes that looked down on her held such restrained fury that for an instant she feared the man was about to do her bodily harm.

"Let me go!" she cried, her voice a mousy squeak. Iron hands tightened their grip on her arms. Danner gave her a shake. She felt the strength of the will that restrained its force and caused him to let out his breath in an exercise of self-control that relaxed his grip. Towering over her, he still pinned her lightly to the wall, powerless to move against him.

"What in the name of frustration do you think you're up to, woman?" he demanded.

It took her a moment to find her voice. When she did, she let her bitterness out undiluted. "You don't care a whit about Glenhaven, and you know it," she accused. "If you really cared, it wouldn't have taken three days for you to decide the matter was worthy of Jules Danner's lofty attention."

He gazed down on her sardonically. "Speak not of which you know naught, Princess," he chided. "I've been on a business trip. I saw your nasty little restraining order for the first time less than an hour ago when I got back from the west coast. Now, I want to know what it's all about."

"I'm not going to let you destroy Glenhaven if I can help it. That's all," she informed him. "If there were any way I could get the place back in the hands of my own family, believe me, that's what I would do. Since I can't, I've turned it over to the historical landmark people. Stop it! You're hurting my arms. Will you kindly let me go?"

For a moment she imagined she saw a flash of bitter humor in his eyes. "Not on your life," he said. "With that temper of yours you might go for my jugular. I would hate to have to deck you, my dear." He relaxed his hold a bit, but his voice was still filled with pent up anger. "That restraining order is a vindictive little piece, Sabrina. Pure dog-in-the-manger. If you can't have Glenhaven yourself, then no one else can. Is that it?"

"That's not true," she cried. "I don't care who has it, as long as it isn't you."

"Me? Why me, especially?"

"The only reason you bought Glenhaven is to shaft the Burkes again."

He let her go then. He stepped back as if he had been struck. From beneath tightly knit brows, the dark, enigmatic eyes glowered down at her.

"For Pete's sake, what is that supposed to mean?" he

asked harshly. Beneath the cold, steady gaze her own faltered. She felt her face grow hot at the thought of giving words to the charges that festered in her mind. He waited.

At last, her voice trembling slightly from emotion, she said, "While I don't know exactly what went on between your father and mine, it's plain to see why you won't tell me the facts—which you obviously know." She hesitated before she continued, choosing her words carefully. "There can be no reason but they make the Danners look bad. This much is clear—your father came out of that partnership rich. I don't have to remind you that mine came out of it a broken, dying man. Need you ask why the thought of Glenhaven in your hands doesn't thrill me with joy?"

There was a sudden stillness about the man and again a change in his eyes. As she raised her own to look into the opaque depths, she imagined she saw a shadow of pain and a new gentleness there.

"So that's it," he said softly. "Who told you this?"

"The evidence is just *there*. Nobody told me," she admitted. "My mother and aunt never talked about it. Somehow it seemed wrong to ask."

"Maybe you should have," Danner suggested quietly.

"Believe me, I intend to, the minute my aunt gets home," Sabrina said. His hand reached out tentatively and touched her shoulder. She shook it off and tried once more to pull away. It was like trying to move against an invisible, invincible force—a magnet, gradually drawing her in. Next moment she was in his arms. His cheek caressed her hair, his voice husky, half-whispering, like a seductive breeze in her ear.

"Sabrina . . . Princess . . . sweet, innocent foolish child. In the name of love, what have those two good women done to you?" His lips touched her forehead, her eyes, her cheeks—her lips; held them in a hungry, possessive kiss.

A passion of yearning swept through her, wave upon wave, deep within, until it seemed she was drowning inside; but in the upper reaches of her mind she understood what the man was up to and resisted. He imagined he had only to make love to her, and she would do anything he asked. *Like withdraw the restraining order! That was his game!* So said her mind, while her body betrayed her and rested dreamily against the sinewy chest. Her ear listened to the sure, fast beat of his heart, and her pulse leaped in response. For a moment she was lost. Then she tore herself from his embrace.

"Stop it," she ordered shakily. "Stop it, at once. If you think you can honey me into giving in to you, think again, Jules Danner!"

He looked down upon her in silence. Then as she still fought for composure, he caught her up in his arms again. His lips pressed down upon hers in a bruising kiss that sent freshets of electric excitement coursing through her body. When finally he released her, she could do nothing but lean upon him, her senses reeling. She regained her control at last and pulled away to face him, her fury reborn in full maturity. The same sardonic smile she had seen before played at one corner of his mouth.

"Give in to me in what respect, Sabrina?" he asked, going back to her own angry words a moment earlier.

"Only insofar as the house is concerned, may I be so bold as to hope?"

She felt her face burst into flame.

"Jules Danner, you *are* despicable," she cried in a choked voice. "The house . . . *everything!* You can't get your way by romancing me, insofar as—oh—*whatever! Don't you understand!* From now on, do us both a favor and don't even bother to try."

She saw his eyes narrow, his face grow tight.

"In that case, there can't be much more for us to say to each other, is there?" he said. Did she hear a note of sadness in his voice or was her imagination reflecting her own sudden strange sorrow as he turned to leave?

He walked away from her toward the front of the shop, his tall, well-balanced body moving coolly, with an easy grace, through the obstacle course of antique pieces that crowded the small store. He opened the door and stepped out, quietly pulling it shut behind him. He went without a word of farewell. He did not look back.

When the plaintive echo of the silver bells died out, a stillness settled over the place. In all her life, Sabrina had never felt so alone.

Chapter Six

Sabrina's program for the next day included a drive downriver some miles to look at a block-front chest its owner claimed to be an authentic eighteenth century American Chippendale made by the Townsend and Goddard craftsmen. Ordinarily, this kind of excursion she looked forward to with pleasure.

This morning she awakened reluctantly. With her eyes still closed, she prejudged the day and decided it was hardly worth getting up for. When she finally ventured a look, the cold, drizzly dawn she saw outside her window seemed a perfect match for her mood.

She realized this didn't make sense. She should have awakened jubilant over yesterday's Glenhaven victory. Hadn't she saved her old home from the wreckers? At least until the landmark people took it under their control, as she had full confidence they would.

So why did she feel so awful, as if she had destroyed

or damaged something infinitely precious beyond repair?

Pulling the covers up over her head, she shut out the morning's dreary light and probed restlessly for a reason for her bleak state of mind. What she found was confusion.

Out of the silence of the warm dark, the voice of Jules Danner came back to her again in his last words of the day before: ". . . there can't be much more for us to say to each other, I suppose."

In a sudden fury she flung off the covers and swung her body to sit upright on the edge of the bed and plant her feet firmly upon the floor. The man was absolutely right, of course. They had nothing more to say to each other. Nothing at all.

She stood up abruptly and headed for the bathroom. There she turned on the shower and stepped under a torrent of hot water. She let the stream pour full force over her head and rush in streaming rivulets off her body, scrubbing herself with a rough sponge until her flesh tingled. Then, as if like *South Pacific*'s Nellie Forbush she could wash the man right out of her hair, she lathered and relathered her head in a froth of shampoo, flushing the suds in stubborn rinsing until all the hot water in the tank ran out.

The morning proved to be even worse than she had anticipated in the early dawn. The block-front chest turned out to be not colonial Vermont but recent Grand Rapids, an ingenious but readily detectable fake. Its owner was quite nasty when Sabrina pointed out the discrepancies and had not taken kindly to her well-meant suggestion that the woman lower both her sights and her price and sell the chest for what it was, a quite good reproduction but no antique.

Sabrina was back at the store before eleven to find the place empty, except for Ethel who was having coffee and doughnuts as she warmed herself at the furnace outlet.

"It's too wet for folks to get out," Ethel opined. "I've had the place to myself. There's a letter from your aunt there on your desk."

"Any phone calls?"

"Mrs. Cotter phoned to say she'd decided to take the Revere compote. She'll be in to pick it up next week. Oh yes, and Ralph Spurling called."

For the first time Sabrina remembered it was Friday again. For a moment she was almost glad that Ralph had not taken her last words to him the week before for the rejection she had meant them to be; but even as she welcomed the prospect of an evening out—even with Ralph—she knew it was no good. Dinner with Jules and Ralph that night a week ago had been the turning point. She knew at last that she could never marry Ralph. It was not fair to use him now. She sighed.

"Am I to call him, or will he call back?" She would tell him on the phone. It would be simpler than face-to-face.

Ethel sniffed disapprovingly and shook her head. "He said he had a dinner date with you tonight, and he called to break it, of all things! Something about the company's big wheels all being in town, and he can't get away. He sounded pretty pleased with himself."

"It's all right, Ethel," Sabrina soothed. "It's a merger or something. Ralph seems to think there's a vice-presidency or something in it for him."

She was really glad for Ralph, she thought absently as she applied the antique letter opener on the desk to Aunt Hat's envelope. If he had to make a choice, he would rather be a vice-president in his insurance company than the husband of Sabrina Burke. It was a new thought that made rejecting him a bit easier to do.

Aunt Hat's letter was typically brief and noncommittal, but it brought the first warm glow to Sabrina's dreary day. Aunt Hat was coming home in just ten days. There would be no need for Sabrina to drive down to Long Island to meet her arriving plane at Kennedy airport.

"An old friend whom I hadn't seen for many years just happens to be on the tour," Aunt Hat wrote. "We've been renewing a warm and pleasant association as we share the wonders of this ancient world. My friend's son will meet us at JFK and drive us up to Sutton. It will save you a trip. Can't wait to see you. Love, Aunt Hat."

Affection for the dear woman who had been her loving confidante for as long as she could remember washed through Sabrina, along with a passing exasperation that her aunt had neglected to mention a meeting with this old friend until the last minute when the trip was all but over. It would have eased her mind to know that two old friends were there to look out for each other. She would have enjoyed thinking of her aunt as one of a pair of middle-aged ladies sharing reminiscences and a rickshaw in the shadow of the Great Wall.

Sabrina's days were now filled with preparations for her aunt's return, leaving little time or energy to pursue the preoccupation with Glenhaven and Jules Danner that had filled her days and haunted her nights in recent weeks. The matter was over and done with, she told herself fiercely when her mind threatened to take it up again as she aired the downstairs garden suite that was her aunt's quarters and scrubbed and polished and scoured until the house and the shop glistened like sun-washed sand.

Still, even in the bustle of such exhausting activity, she could not completely divest herself of the effects of the bruising days she had lived through since Jules came into her life. One day she gave in to a growing curiosity to see if anything was happening at Glenhaven, now that the restraining order had gone into effect, and drove down the road to the old place one late afternoon.

She felt a stir of shameful excitement, half-expecting to find the gate open and Jules Danner's Mercedes parked in the circular driveway; but it was not to be. She was ashamed of the nagging disappointment that came over her when she saw the lock. Over the high stone wall she could see nothing of the mansion but its rooftops. There was a graveyard stillness about the place that told her it was deserted—except, perhaps, for the ghosts of the old betrayal, she thought wryly.

Glenhaven wasn't the only place that looked neglected, thought Sabrina next morning as she stepped outside the shop to see how the window boxes had fared after the first fall storm. Except for a layer of leaves and debris that had blown in around the plants, the flowers looked bright and healthy; but the yard and walks were buried under a thick blanket of sodden leaves. Her first act when she got inside was to call a local gardening service to send a man to clean up the mess.

Three hours later, when Sabrina went into the kitchen to fix lunch for herself, she found that Hero was gone. She remembered then, with a sinking feeling in her stomach, that it had completely slipped her mind to warn the new gardener about the red-gold dog and the gate.

She called the animal shelter at once to put them on notice that once again her truant had slipped away; then she set out on foot to comb the neighborhood, not really expecting to find him that easily. More likely, before the day was over the shelter would call her to come and get the dog. As the afternoon wore on, however, and no call came, her concern gradually grew until by nightfall when the animal was still missing, a pall of worry settled over her.

When a second day passed, and the dog had still not been turned in at the shelter, Sabrina was genuinely alarmed. She remembered the awful moment she'd seen him dodging cars on the busy thoroughfare past Glenhaven and called the local and state police to be on watch for a red-gold dog along the road. Sick with anxiety over the lost pet, she turned the store over to Ethel and Dora and took to the roads herself in her small station wagon, hoping in vain that her eye might catch a glimpse of the tawny retriever bounding across some country field.

By the fourth day when she made her morning calls to the authorities, she had all but given up hope—especially after the man at the shelter gave her a new worry when he said that strangers passing through had been known to load dogs into their cars and make off with them.

With a feeling of hopelessness, she closed the shop early that afternoon and set out once more on her hunt.

Turning into the four-lane arterial a few blocks from the store, Sabrina was suddenly aware of a cream-colored Mercedes ahead of her, traveling in the direction she was going. Her heart quickened. Almost in spite of herself, her foot went heavy on the gas pedal, and a moment later she was near enough to see the straight set of broad, muscular shoulders and well-shaped head with its splendid mane of dark brown hair that told her the driver was Jules Danner. Without knowing why, she continued across the intersection where she had planned to turn off and moved along, a car-length behind him, as if an invisible towline was fastened between their two cars. At the same time her mind was working furiously as she tried to justify the crazy impulse that caused her to follow his car.

Hero! Maybe Jules Danner had seen Hero somewhere. It wouldn't hurt to find out. She might as well just stay with him until she got his attention and signal him to pull over to the side. Her pulse raced madly at the thought of the bold thing she was about to do.

Danner drove swiftly. It was not long before Sabrina sensed some grim purpose in the speed and skill with which he maneuvered the vehicle, and she quickly lost the feeling her car was being pulled by his. It was all she could do, in fact, to keep up with him in the space behind.

As the green light at the traffic signal a short distance ahead turned to amber, she saw the opportunity to pull into the lane beside the Mercedes. When Danner came to a stop, she could give him a beep of her horn; then, as she was about to do just that, it crossed her mind that he could very well give her a cold stare and cruise arrogantly on his way. The thought stayed her hand.

Approaching the intersection ahead of her, the Mercedes came to a quick stop as the signal light turned red. Pulling up in the adjoining lane, Sabrina asked herself what she was thinking of. This piece of foolishness had nothing to do with Hero. She might as well be honest with herself. What she had been about to do was a straight play for Jules Danner's attention and nothing else.

In self-searching reproof, she faced a new fact about herself: whatever attention she got from Danner—whether it be hostile or warm—had come to mean more to her than pure admiration from any other man.

Trapped now in traffic, Sabrina wanted only to escape unobserved before Jules Danner saw her for the fool she was. She scrunched down behind her wheel unobtrusively and prayed for the light to change before his eyes fell on her. Nevertheless, at the very last moment when the light was ready to change, she couldn't resist a quick glance to her left.

He looked straight ahead, preoccupied and quite unaware of her presence, she saw; plainly impatient. Relieved, she turned her eyes back to wait for the signal change. It was then she caught a glimpse of the red-gold dog lying in the seat beside him. The next instant the light turned green, and the Mercedes shot ahead; but not before Sabrina, reticence forgotten, craned her neck for a better look and satisfied herself that Jules Danner was making off with Hero. Neither home nor the animal shelter were in the direction he sped.

She was paralyzed for a moment with the shock of the discovery. Not until cars behind her began to honk did she pull herself together and take off in a belated burst of speed in a futile effort to catch up with the Mercedes already far ahead. When she lost sight of the vehicle at last in traffic, she pulled off at the next intersection and gave up the chase.

Driving slowly home, Sabrina puzzled furiously over the strange situation. What on earth was the man up to? People just didn't go off with other people's pets. Oh, some larcenous stranger, perhaps; but not a man of Jules Danner's ilk.

The more she thought of it, the more convinced she became that Danner was deliberately hiding the dog to get back at her for the restraining order. From the first meeting with the man she had known he would be a strong adversary, but she had never thought he would stoop to petty malice to even scores.

By the time she reached home, Sabrina had worked herself into a fine lather of fury. When she remembered the nights she had tossed in sleepless worry over the dog, the anxious days she'd spent hunting him, she wanted with all the power of her pent up frustration to make Jules Danner pay. Maybe there wasn't any statute that dealt specifically with dog-napping, but there were laws against malicious mischief and outright thievery. She intended to put them to use.

She hurried up the stairs. Leaving her coat on a living room chair, she headed for the window seat that looked out upon the street. There she sat down and reached for the phone on a small table off to one side. She was about to dial when suddenly the momentum of anger that had propelled her to this point slowed down. She hesitated. Did she really want her personal battle with Jules Danner to wind up in the hands of the police? Did she want it advertised in the press—*Head of Electronics Company Arrested for Stealing Pet*—to become the gossip of Dutchess County?

Somewhat calmer now, though still seething with indignation, she gazed thoughtfully out the window, down on the street below. She watched the roof of a dark blue car as it approached and passed, following it with her eyes to the corner at the end of the block where it turned out of sight. She glanced at her watch. It was after five. Uncle George might still be at his office; she knew his habits. Some days he came in late, and when he did, he was scrupulously late going home. She dialed. Luck was with her. Instead of his secretary, George Channing himself answered the phone.

"Uncle George—" she began hesitantly.

"Sabrina! What's on your mind, child?"

"It's Jules Danner again," she told him, making every effort to keep her voice calm. "He's taken Hero, my golden retriever."

There was a moment of silence before the old lawyer's voice came crackling back across the line. "We've got a bad connection, child. It sounded like you just said Jules had run off with your dog."

"Please, Uncle George! That's what I *did* say. I'm serious," she cried, almost in tears.

"All right. I'm sorry," the old gentleman said with a sigh. "Tell me about it, honey. What's Jules doing with your dog?"

"Who knows?" said Sabrina unhappily. "Trying to get even with me, I suppose."

"You know for sure Jules has got him?"

"I saw him. Hero was in the front seat of his car, riding around the country with him. The dog's been missing for four days. I've been going crazy, looking for him," she said. Then on a note of further desperation, "Aunt Hat will be home Thursday. She gave the dog to me. I've got to get Hero back before then."

"Harriet's coming home Thursday, you say?"

"Yes."

There was a long pause. Finally the old attorney said, "Sabrina, honey, I'd just wait for Harriet to get home, if I were you. It'll all work out. The dog's in good hands. You don't want to do something you'll be sorry for."

"But Uncle George—," she wailed.

"Now you listen to me, Sabrina. There's been some kind of a mistake. Just hold your horses, and wait."

"There's no mistake, Uncle George," she cried stubbornly. "I saw him making off with my dog. I saw it with my own eyes."

"Then call the police, child," George Channing said, his patience clearly at an end. "The matter's not for me."

As the old lawyer spoke Sabrina noticed in the failing light outside the window, a cream-colored car rounding the corner to enter the block below, moving rapidly up the tree-lined street. As it reached the house it braked and turned unexpectedly into her driveway. She drew a quick breath, only half-hearing the old man's last words. It was Jules Danner's Mercedes.

"Never mind, Uncle George," she said, her voice suddenly weak. "I'm sorry I bothered you. Let's just let it ride."

"That's more like it," the lawyer said approvingly.

"You're a good girl, Sabrina. A good girl but inclined to be impetuous. Give my regards to Harriet when she arrives."

With a quick good-bye to the old gentleman, Sabrina put down the phone, her pulse pounding fiercely. A moment later the doorbell rang and she ran down to turn on the porch light against the gathering dusk before she opened the door.

He stood in the circle of light, the tall, ruggedly handsome man, his face stern and uncompromising. In spite of her anger, a shock of excitement coursed through her body, but she kept herself rigidly in hand. With cold restraint, as if to an unwelcome stranger, she said, "Yes?"

"I have your dog," Jules Danner told her in a voice of stinging reproof that brought a wave of heat to her cheeks.

"I know," she snapped, "and if you don't return him at once, I shall call the police."

The deep blue eyes stared down at her with a look of frosty disbelief. "Police? What the devil are you talking about?"

"You know what I'm talking about," she accused. *What you're up to!*—that's what I'm talking about. Don't think I don't know. You'll give back Hero, if I'll agree to have the restraining order lifted. Isn't that it? Well, let me tell you, Jules Danner, I'll do no such thing. I'll call the police first."

She saw the strong jaw tighten and set in a disdainful line. Her pulse raced madly as she braced herself for a storm. Then to her astonishment, Jules Danner turned on his heel and stalked down the driveway toward where he had left his car. Darkness had settled in, but she could see the strong line of the man's broad shoulders as he walked away from her out of the light, the imperious set of his head.

Her anger gave way to bewilderment. She heard the car door open, and after a moment close again. He was running off with Hero again, and she was powerless to stop him.

She was turning back into the house, the police again in her mind, when out of the darkness at the end of the driveway, Jules Danner came back into the circle of light from the porch. In his arms he carried the great body of the golden retriever, like a hurt child.

Sabrina's first thought was that the animal was dead.

"Hero!" she cried. She ran forward with arms outstretched as if to snatch the dog from Danner. "What have you done to him?"

Her hand touched the animal's head, and she saw a feeble twitch of the tail. There was no break in Danner's stride as he moved on past her up the steps to the porch, ignoring her outstretched arms.

"We've made it this far," he said caustically over his shoulder. "Would you mind just showing me where you want him to go and let me take him the rest of the way?"

Sabrina's face went warm. Of course there was no way she could have carried the big creature without Danner, he weighed almost as much as she did, but the man didn't have to go out of his way to make her feel foolish!

She brushed past Danner and opened the door, leading the way across the entrance hall and into the kitchen, determined to establish that here she was in charge as she stood by to let the man lay his burden down gently on the rug where Hero customarily slept. Sabrina dropped to her knees beside the animal, half weeping with relief as she saw a glimmer of joyful recognition in the dull eyes. The golden plume lifted and fell against the floor in a feeble imitation of a wag.

"Oh Hero, Hero!" she cried, laying her face lovingly against the big dog's head. Next moment she was on her feet, glaring angrily at the man who stood by, watching the scene with a strange look on his face.

"You've got a lot of explaining to do, Jules Danner," she said furiously. "What have you done to Hero?"

The dark, inscrutable eyes gazed down at her for a long moment of silence before he spoke. "May I suggest you're hardly the one to take a carping tone in the matter, Sabrina. The dog wouldn't be in the shape he's in if you kept better tabs on him."

"If you're accusing me of neglect, forget it," Sabrina flared. She hadn't gone through four days of worry and self-reproach to endure further flagellation from the man who had compounded her woes. "The dog got away, and yes, I'm at fault, but you didn't have to load him into your car and make off with him. I worried myself sick. If you had just let him alone, someone would have turned him in at the animal shelter, and they would notify me. You used him as a pawn to get even with me! It's *your* fault he got hit by a car or—well—here you bring him home—half dead—" In the middle of her tirade, something snapped into place in her mind. She broke off with a gasp and looked up at the man beside her with stricken eyes.

Wry-voiced, Danner picked up on it. "That's the girl! Give old Jules the benefit of the doubt."

"Oh, my word," she whispered sickly. "What *did*

happen? Will he be all right? Shouldn't we get him to the vet?"

Coldly, sarcastically Danner replied, "I thought you'd never ask. Yes, he'll be all right. He's full of antibiotics and doped up with pain-killer at the moment. We just got back from the vet. He'll survive. In a day or two he'll be his old self."

So that's where the Mercedes had been headed when she'd seen him earlier, thought Sabrina, all at once unsure of herself. In a small voice, she asked, "How long have you had him?"

Danner made a conspicuous play of looking at his watch. "About an hour and twenty-seven minutes, give or take a second or two."

Again Sabrina felt completely abashed. Uncle George was right. He hadn't stolen the dog. Unable any more to meet the cutting gaze of the man who looked down on her, she turned her eyes away.

"I—I thought—"

"I know what you thought," Jules Danner said severely, "and far be it from me to spoil your pleasure in my villainous image by explaining my part in the case of the missing dog." He turned abruptly and headed for the door.

Before Sabrina found her voice he was almost out of the kitchen. "Wait!" she cried. "Please tell me what happened. I want to know the whole thing."

He hesitated, then relenting turned back. "I can't tell you any more than I know," he said reasonably, but with an edge of resentment still there. "I found him about four-thirty this afternoon, locked in at Glenhaven and in pretty bad shape. He'd picked up a burr and his foot was badly infected. I could tell the poor devil was running a fever. He was a sick dog, so I took him to the vet before bringing him back to you."

"How long do you think he'd been locked up?"

"I've no idea. I just got back from the coast. Since the first day you lost him, I'd guess," Jules said. "He was starved but he parked himself next to water, the one thing he couldn't survive without. He'd got next to a broken sprinkler-head with a puddle. That's where I found him, waiting for someone to rescue him."

Sabrina shook her head, mystified. "I don't see how he got in. That's the first place I went. I checked the fence, myself. There's not a chink big enough for him to squeeze through."

"I'd guess he got in while the contractor was there," Jules told her. There was a flash of anger in the deep blue eyes as he continued caustically, "When you put us out of business, the contractor got a key from me to pick up some sawhorses and stuff he'd left in the house. The dog must have slipped through the gate after him and laid low so the contractor didn't discover him when he locked up."

"Any place else Hero would have turned up at the animal shelter before the day was over," Sabrina said crossly. "He would have to pick Glenhaven!"

"Of course. Isn't that where he always goes?" asked Danner in exasperation. "This isn't the first time he's run away, you know. I'm the one who turns him in at the shelter since I bought Glenhaven awhile back. I don't know who he visited before that."

"But I thought—"

"Blast it, Princess, you don't control your thoughts

113

any better than you control your dog," Danner barked. "He's been out to Glenhaven on his own five or six times since—"

"But the animal shelter—"

"That's where I took him before I found out who he belonged to. He was underfoot a lot, I might add. When I saw he was to be a regular visitor, I decided it was time somebody taught him to obey," Jules said, his voice goading again. "It looks like he wants to be mastered. I've even found him in front of the locked gate waiting to be let in."

"I don't know what you are talking about," said Sabrina stiffly. "He couldn't behave better around the house."

Danner gave a derisive laugh. "And like a complete renegade when he gets out. The day you came into Glenhaven after him, you couldn't get him to do anything, and you know it. He wouldn't stay. He wouldn't sit. He wouldn't come. You notice, he minded me."

The gibe stung. She hadn't forgotten the arrogance with which Jules had taken command of the dog that day. She had been mystified and embarrassed. Now she was mad. He might have had the decency to explain. She was furious to learn now that he had been enjoying a mean little joke at her expense all the while.

She was not one to weep, but the four days of anxiety and sleeplessness had taken their toll. To her horror she feared she was about to burst into tears in the face of Jules Danner, a humiliation she felt she could not survive. She turned her head away and summoned all her control in an effort to steady herself.

"I should have guessed from the first that you had

been working to win him over to you," she said. Her voice broke. It didn't come off—the contempt she had intended to convey. She took a step to escape, but Jules reached out quickly and barred the way.

Suddenly gentle, he cupped his hands beneath the curve of her chin and with a consummate tenderness that sent the held-back tears spilling out, he stroked her cheeks and took her face in his hands and tipped it up to his, holding it there for a long moment, as if memorizing what he saw. At last he laid a kiss, hardly more than a whisper of one, on each eyelid.

She had no strength to move. She stood as if hypnotized while he let go of her and reached into a pocket to pull out an immaculate while linen handkerchief and dried her tears. He kissed her face softly, then with a small, involuntary groan, he crushed her into his arms and held her there.

"Oh Sabrina, Sabrina," he said, his voice quiet as he released her, "are we destined to quarrel forever?"

He stayed only a moment after that. Like a caress, he put a hand on her shoulder and guided her into the hallway and pointed her up the stairs.

"Up you go," he said. "You're exhausted. Take a long soak in a tub and get yourself ready for bed." It was a firm order. She had no will but to obey.

With a last light kiss on her lips, he urged her gently away from him up the stairs.

"Good-night, sweet Princess," he said. She was too bemused to reply.

Chapter Seven

In a state of languor, Sabrina climbed the stairs to her room and set about doing what Jules had directed, like an obedient child. For the first time she realized she was very tired, but with the tiredness there was a strange, mindless contentment she savored dreamily, careful to avoid all thought as to its source.

She soaked in the tub until the skin on her hands and feet was pale and puckery, and the water had gone lukewarm. She was dry and comfortably wrapped in the old silk quilted robe when the doorbell rang downstairs. Wondering who it could be at this time of night, she was of half a mind to let it go until she remembered that "this time of night" was really only a little past seven. So much had happened in so short a time it had seemed for a moment like midnight.

She moved lazily out to the landing at the top of the

stairs and switched on the porch light. Through the one-way glass at the side of the door below, she saw that her visitor was Jules, and her heart leaped with joy at his return. She skimmed down the stairs to welcome him, reminded again as she flung open the door and saw him standing there, arms full of mysterious boxes and bags, a boyish grin on his face, what a remarkably handsome man he was.

"Jules!" she said breathlessly. "What are you doing here?"

"I brought a peace offering. May I come in?"

The largest box in his arms, marked with the logo of Sutton's very good catering service, reminded her forcefully that she'd had nothing to eat for many hours. *He remembered she should be fed!* she thought incredulously and purred like a kitten inside. She could find no words to express her pleasure, but when she looked into the face turned down to hers and thanked him with her eyes, it seemed not to matter that he'd caught her speechless. He followed her up the stairs and into the little butler's pantry where he laid down his armload of bundles and brought out from among them a chilled bottle of white wine.

"How about a corkscrew?" he asked, and when she produced one from a drawer, "Oh, and wine glasses and all that other stuff. Silverware—dishes—you know."

She brought out two Waterford wine glasses from the Sheraton breakfront in the small dining room, and while Jules opened the bottle with the ease and finesse of an experienced winemaster, she set the table for two with family Haviland and heirloom silver on Irish

117

embroidered linen doilies that had been her Grandmother Glendon's.

The wine poured, Jules handed her a glass and
touched it lightly with his, crystal to crystal bringing
forth a clear, sweet sound—like a bell. Over the rims of
the glasses the violet eyes looked into the midnight blue
eyes deeply and searchingly for a long moment before
they drank. The ritual of the silent toast completed,
Jules took Sabrina's arm and guided her out of the
pantry, through the dining room to the love seat by the
fire in the living room. There they sipped their wine and
watched the flame patterns—she, in her weariness,
content to let the bewildering mixture of emotions
within her, asleep for a moment, stay at rest. As for
Jules, *well, who knows what goes on in the mind of Jules
Danner?* she asked herself, with a surreptitious, half-
shy glance to see if she could guess.

Catching her eyes on him, Jules emerged from his
own reverie to take her hand and examine it thoughtfully for a moment before he turned it over, laid a kiss in
her palm and folded her fingers over the spot where his
lips had touched. He left her to stoke the fire and put a
stack of records on the turntable, taking her wine glass
from her and putting it on the mantel beside his own
upon return.

With a flourishing bow and a grand gesture that
parodied a headwaiter he said, "May I have the pleasure of seating Madame at her table?" And before she
could protest, had she the will to do so, Jules picked her
up in his arms and kneeling, set her lightly down on the
carpeted floor by the coffee table. He filled her wine
glass from the bottle in an ice-bucket beside the table.

"Madame's waiter will be with her shortly," he

informed her and departed, with another courtly bow, for the pantry.

Sabrina curled up contentedly like a cat and let the sweet, haunting strains of Debussy wash over her while she sipped her wine. In a moment Jules was back to set a place for her where she sat at the low table in front of the fire. He laid a single long-stemmed red rose upon the napkin and beside it a card engraved with the name of Jules Danner, his face blandly innocent as he turned away toward the pantry again.

Sabrina breathed deeply of the rose and read the message written in a bold hand across the back of the card: *"Princess—How about peace and a new beginning?"*

Hungrily, as if it had the properties of the poppy, she breathed in the fragrance of the rose again and emptied her wine glass absently for the second time with no thought to how it might affect her on an empty stomach and in her exhausted condition. She was suddenly wonderfully light-headed and lighthearted. *Why not peace?* she asked herself dreamily; and in answer put the thought aside to think about tomorrow. Tonight she would think of Jules only as a man for all seasons who could stage this playful performance—as delightfully mannered as a minuet—yet could throw himself on an attacker when called upon with all the primitive power of a Tarzan defending his Jane.

She turned a smile of delighted appreciation upon Jules, returning at the moment with her dinner. At her look of welcome, he quickened his step and set the Haviland plate on the table before her. Hands free, he dropped to the floor beside her and pulled her to him. She closed her eyes and savored the soft, sensuous press of his mouth as it covered hers. His hands moved with a kind of urgency across her shoulders and arms as if seeking to define the body beneath the silken robe.

In her euphoria, Sabrina reached up and touched Jules's face, pulling it down to give her lips to him again when he let her go. As if it were the most natural act in the world, she slipped her arms over his shoulder and cradled herself to him until he gave a small moan and unclasped her hands gently from around his neck.

"Princess . . . Princess . . ." he said hoarsely. It seemed he could not go on. He put her away from him and got to his feet where he stood looking down at her with a rueful smile.

"Sabrina, wonderful child, you mustn't count on more restraint from this mortal man than he has the will to exercise," he said softly.

She whispered in answer, "Jules, I am not a child."

Jules said in a strained voice, "Praise be, you're not!" Then with a nod toward the dinner he had put before her, he murmured, *"Bon appétit."* For the first time Sabrina saw that he had set only one place at the table.

"But you're having dinner with me," she protested. She was halfway to her feet when Jules laid a light hand on her shoulder and pressed her down again.

"Not tonight, Princess. You are very tired and need to be alone. Besides, if I stayed I could never leave," he said. She was surprised at the intensity of his last words.

He bent down to drop a light kiss on the crown of her head. "Don't move. I'll look in on the invalid animal on my way out and pop a pill in his mouth, so there'll be no need for you to go down. Eat your dinner and go to bed. Good-night little Princess. 'Parting is such sweet sorrow.' "

Yearning, Sabrina watched him go. After a moment she addressed herself obediently to the Haviland plate on which was a plump squab, butterflied and broiled, fresh French-cut green beans with a dash of tarragon, a lightly tossed salad of butter lettuce and a perfect *baba au rhum* for dessert.

Curled up on the carpet beside the low table, she sipped the wine and savored the superb food to the very last morsel, charmed not only by its quality and flavor but by the elegant restraint shown by the man in selecting it.

It was not in Jules's nature to show off with an expensive French-labeled bottle from some celebrated chateau but to compliment her with the implied assumption she would recognize the excellence of the California wine he had chosen for her. Nor had he tried to overwhelm her with an elaborate floral offering— just a single red rose.

At the same time, the succulent little broiled bird was the real thing, no Rock Cornish game hen—a poor man's substitute—but genuine squab, as costly these days as truffles and as rare as larks' tongues. Nothing but his own fine and sensitive instincts, she mused as she took the first bite, could have told him it was one of her favorite foods.

When she had eaten the last, delicious dab of the *baba,* she pushed the dishes aside and slumped down to cushion her head drowsily on her arms at the table and listen to the lovely closing passages of *Daphnis and Chloë.* When the music had spun to a close, she lay there for a time, the haunting strains still singing in her head, until at last she forced herself to her feet.

Minutes later, she was in bed asleep.

In the initial moments of full awakening, the rainbow wisps of last night's dreamlike events drifted swiftly away, and Sabrina was aware of nothing but a dull, throbbing headache. Outside, a new rain slanted across her window. Raising herself gingerly in deference to her cranky head, she sat up in bed and wondered if she were coming down with something.

Could it have been the wine? No. Not that, she decided. A glass or two of wine had never given her any problems. Whatever it was, she felt rotten.

There was a nagging drumbeat over her right temple as she slipped into the citron-colored robe and cautiously made her way into the living room. The sight that met her eyes filled her with dismay—all the leftovers of the last evening's diversions waiting to be cleaned up. Across the room a small light on the front of the turntable component glowed reproachfully, telling her she had neglected to shut off the stereo system when the last record played out.

Turning it off, she walked over to the coffee table with its clutter of unwashed dishes and the bare, fragile skeleton of last night's plump squab. She looked down on the clutter in disgust, reminding herself that she had been terribly tired; but even as she came up with this quite respectable excuse, she reached down and picked up the uncorked wine bottle and held it up to the light. Her heavy eyelids flew up in surprise.

At least she wasn't coming down with anything, she thought disdainfully. She, who had never imbibed more than two or three glasses of wine in an evening before, had sipped away a full bottle at one sitting, except for the one glass Jules had poured for himself at first. *Congratulations!* she said to herself grimly. *Now you know how a hangover feels.*

In an act of chastisement, she swept up the remains of her private repast and carried the dishes through the dining room to the pantry, setting them in the dumbwaiter that sent them to the kitchen to be washed. She snatched the single red rose, now withered and shrunken on the coffee table where it lay forgotten, and crumpled it in her hand.

Jules Danner had bewitched her! She'd succumbed again to his devilish charms. She'd let him go away smugly assured that she would give in to whatever he asked when he came back to press his claim. And come back he would, if she read the message on his card with the rose rightly. She picked it up from the table where it lay and read again, ". . . peace and a new beginning?" She tore the card into confetti pieces and scattered them over the last dying embers from the fire of the night before.

Oh yes, he'd be back, all right! He had planned it well. After last night's subtle softening he would be back to suggest she lift the restrictions on Glenhaven. If necessary, he would woo her falsely again. The wine, the squab, the single red rose—that, of course, was what they were about.

He'd be back, she told herself bitterly, but this time she would be strong. There would be no more tender moments for Jules Danner to build on. No more! Never again!

Stepping out on the landing, she was relieved to find

Hero at the foot of the stairs looking up at her with a pair of wistful eyes, whimpering softly for her to descend.

In the kitchen she made herself eat a single poached egg, a piece of toast and a cup of coffee. She popped two aspirin in her mouth, gulped a full glass of water, wrestled a capsule down Hero's unwilling throat and went across the hall into the store to wind the clocks.

"You all right, Sabrina? You worrying about the dog?" Ethel asked a short time later when she walked in to find Sabrina huddled at her desk in the alcove, eyes closed, hands pressed glumly over her ears. "You look kinda green around the gills. What's the matter with you?"

She had a perverse impulse to say, "Sorry. I've got a hangover"; but the quick picture of Ethel's mouth, pinched tight in disapproval, caused Sabrina to stifle the urge.

"No. I feel fine," she lied. "Hero's back home." She didn't feel like elaborating.

Ethel said, "That's nice."

As was too often the case in the first wet days of autumn, business was slow. After the first hour Sabrina left the salesroom to Ethel and withdrew to her alcove. There on the other side of the oriental screen she did penance by keeping her eyes resolutely on her work, resisting the temptation to desert her post whenever the silver bells at the front door signaled the arrival of a customer.

The aspirin had rid her of the headache but had done nothing for her state of mind. Though she half-expected Jules Danner to appear, when, after a long silence in the shop the bells rang and she heard the man's cheerful baritone wish a pleasant good morning to Ethel out front, it was all she could do not to panic.

"My name is Jules Danner," she heard him introduce himself to Ethel in his most ingratiating voice. "Miss Burke may have told you I found her golden retriever yesterday in rather a bad condition. He's been seen by a vet, but I thought I'd like to check in with her this morning and see how the old fellow's making it today."

"Oh, *you're* the one that brought poor Hero back," Ethel twittered. In her hideaway behind the screen Sabrina muttered glumly, *"Stop drooling, Ethel."*

"Sabrina was half sick with worry," Ethel confided. "She's more than grateful, I'm sure."

"Is Miss Burke in?"

"Oh yes, and dying to see you, I know. Come right along with me."

Before Sabrina could do more than breathe a silent word of protest, a beaming Ethel was there, looking over the tambour desk, with Jules Danner right behind her. The plump, little middle-aged woman was clearly entranced by the tall, rugged man who looked every inch the country gentleman this morning in a fine muted beige and gray plaid shirt worn under a shearling jacket with tan whipcord pants and Wellington boots, all beaded with rain.

"Mr. Danner is here to see about Hero, Sabrina," Ethel announced with such a flourish Sabrina thought she was about to curtsy.

"I see," said Sabrina curtly.

"Go show him the dog, honey," Ethel directed. "I'll mind the store." The front bell jingled, and she backed off around the screen. "I'll go. Take your time. I'll take care of things out there."

"Nice lady," Jules Danner commented.

"Ethel? She thinks she owns the place *and* me. She looks on herself as my foster mother," said Sabrina in exasperation. "She came to work here for my aunt when she was right out of high school. She's been here nearly as long as the shop."

"Still a nice lady," said Danner.

"Of course she is," said Sabrina impatiently, ashamed that she'd disposed of Ethel so carelessly. "She's a dear. She's like my own family. It's just —" She hesitated, not sure what she intended to say.

"It's just that you wish she hadn't led me into your inner sanctum, isn't that right?" Jules teased.

Sabrina's headache was coming back. If only he wouldn't make her feel like such a ninny. She prayed for a snappy rejoinder, but there was nothing on her tongue but a bad taste.

"Don't worry. I didn't come to steal the tambour desk out from under you," he assured her with a wicked grin, "but watch out for Rhonda. She's here in the Sutton area on a scouting trip for antiques today. She's determined to have your desk. If I were you, I'd lock it up and hide the key."

"You can tell Ms. Bartlett for me that she's wasting her time," Sabrina informed him shortly, with a sinking heart. She had been right in the beginning. Glenhaven was only a part of Danner's relationship with the decorator. Though work there had come to a halt for an indefinite time, that didn't stop them from seeing each other, it would appear.

Danner laughed. "When I see her, I'll tell her," he

said. "But I didn't come here to discuss Rhonda. I came to see how the patient's doing."

Uncertain whether the remark referred to Hero or was intended as an oblique reference to her own sorry state the night before, Sabrina chose not to risk a wrong interpretation. "Hero is quite himself this morning, thank you, and so am I," she said with a sweet, formal politeness that acknowledged the requirements of common courtesy, yet she hoped made it clear that his charming and elaborate ploy of the previous evening had changed nothing between them. "You were more than kind to go to such a lot of trouble for both Hero and me. I am indeed obliged to you."

Danner eyed her quizzically for a moment. "In that case, come down off your high horse, Princess, and tell me what's wrong with things now."

How she hated his calling her *Princess!* The word fell on her ears each time like an accusation, as if Jules Danner imagined she considered herself someone special, a cut above the rest of the world. She looked on the word as a snide put-down, as cruel as it was unfair.

She said stiffly, "I'm sure I don't know what you are talking about. Now, if you came to see Hero . . ." She stood up and walked away from the desk, conscious that he watched her curiously as she leaned around the screen and spoke to Ethel to let her know she was about to leave.

She was acutely aware of Danner's presence only a step behind her. Head high and back plumb line straight, she led the way across the hall to the kitchen. To her chagrin Hero, languishing on his rug, leaped up to greet Danner in an ecstasy of delight, gamboling foolishly about on three feet to welcome him.

"Steady boy," Danner said quietly. The words brought the big dog to an immediate halt in front of the man, who dropped down on one knee to examine the injured paw. "Nasty sore, but it seems to be clearing up well enough," he commented. Rising to his feet, he reached down to run an affectionate hand over the tawny coat. "Thanks for the warm greeting, old friend. I'm glad *your* good humor hasn't gone sour," he said, and then, still to the dog, "Is it my imagination, or do you feel a certain chill in the air?"

Sabrina ignored the side glance her way and turned to leave. "If you're quite satisfied Hero is not suffering from neglect at my hands, I really must get back to the store," she said tartly.

"Now Sabrina. Back up, lady," ordered Danner. He laid a delaying hand on her arm. She steeled herself against the thrill that raced through her body at his touch.

Here we go again, she told herself in bitter irony. The next moment she would be in his arms. He would kiss her, his hands caress her as he pulled her close. The temptation to let it happen nearly overwhelmed her. She reminded herself sternly that Jules Danner was using her again; only this time she would cut him down coolly and with dignity. She would not let him goad her into a quarrel, only to find herself scolding at him like a fishwife. Even as she made these vows, she fought to control the silly breathlessness that came with the touch of his hand. She did not jerk away or try to escape from him this time. She let his hand stay where it was, neither resisting nor encouraging, though it seemed to burn a brand into her flesh. She looked at him, politely questioning.

Danner continued in haste, "Wait a minute, won't you. There's something I have to discuss with you."

"I think not," she said in a level voice. "As far as I'm concerned, we've already said it all."

With an air or perplexity, the man shook his head. "Blast it, Sabrina," he exclaimed, "one minute you blow hot and the next you blow cold." A hot denial at what she considered an unfair charge rose to her lips, but he gave her no chance to voice it.

He said placatingly, "Never mind about that. We'll speak of your foibles another time. What I'm concerned about at the moment is that jungle of underbrush out there at Glenhaven."

Sabrina stared at him in astonishment, at a loss to find a reason why he would discuss the Glenhaven underbrush with her. "I really have to go," she protested. "I told Ethel I'd be right back, and she may—"

"Knock it off, Sabrina," Danner said in a weary tone. "There's not a customer in the store. It's raining buckets outside. If you are really concerned about Glenhaven, you'll take five minutes to listen to me."

"Of course I'm concerned," said Sabrina indignantly, "but I don't see what the condition of the Glenhaven grounds has to do with me."

"Just this: it presents all kinds of problems. You know what it's like. Wild vines and brush choking the trees and plantings, dead branches falling all over the place. It's a haven for vagrants and fugitives, as you have reason to recall, although that's not my main concern at the moment."

Mystified, Sabrina said uncertainly, "You don't have to tell me. It's a mess, but I don't know what you want me to do about it at this late date."

129

"I want you to alter that restraining order. The grounds are not just a mess, they are a fire hazard. It's got to be cleared out, but the way you've got it tied up we can't touch it," Danner said forcefully. "You'll have to get George Channing to modify the order so we can get on with what has to be done."

A sick disappointment settled like a rock in the pit of Sabrina's stomach. So she was right! This was the reason for Jules Danner's pretty advances. What a fool she had been! Until this moment she hadn't truly believed—had half convinced herself, in fact, that the man was falling in love with her; had even gone so far as to look blindly for an honorable resolution to the family bitterness that endangered a romantic relationship with him.

A fullness in her throat kept her from giving voice to her outrage for a moment. "You're out of your mind," she said at last dully, the pain of disillusionment quenching the immediate fire of her wrath.

Danner looked at her in surprise. "I wouldn't say that. If I don't get at it before it dries up after the rain, that appraisal might be fair. Come on, Sabrina. Quit sparring. I've got a real fire hazard out there."

"Fire hazard? After this kind of rain!" Sabrina managed to scoff.

"These early rains dry off in a couple of days, and the weatherbirds are predicting an unusually dry fall. I'd like to get started tomorrow," Danner said reasonably; then, clearly losing all patience, "Don't be so damn hardheaded! I'm asking you to get on that phone to George Channing *now—if you don't mind,*" he finished with deadly sarcasm.

In the heat of her anger and the depths of pain, all

thought of coolness and dignity were lost. Sabrina lashed out at him, "You *are* a scoundrel, Jules Danner. I *do* mind. I mind very much. I'm not about to have that order changed."

Danner stared at her in disbelief. "You can't mean that, Sabrina. The place could turn into a tinderbox out there. Be reasonable. I thought you loved your old home."

"I do love it. I just don't believe you, that's all," said Sabrina coldly.

This time it was Danner whose temper flared. "Now wait a minute—"

Sabrina broke in, "I think you made it all up—about the hazards of fire. You think you'll keep hacking away at that restraining order a little bit at a time until there's nothing left to stand in your way. If it's such a fire hazard, why haven't you done something about it before?"

He was furious, she knew, but when he answered there was no sign in his voice of the heat she saw in his eyes. "That's a fair enough question," he said evenly. "All I can say is that I thought the grounds should wait until the work on the house was done, and I didn't give them any thought. I really looked at the problem for the first time yesterday when I found the dog there. I admit, I asked myself the same question. The point is, no harm's been done, that is, if you'll just forget you've got it in for me long enough to get that restraining order modified."

"Don't think I can't recognize a typical Danner trick when I see one," she said scornfully. Then, as his fingers tightened on her arm, "And don't bother to sweep me off my feet. It won't work anymore."

For a foolish instant she thought she saw in the dark eyes a pain to match her own; but then they were veiled, and she could read nothing in them at all. He released his grip on her arms.

"*Why*, Sabrina?" he asked quietly. "It's only to protect the old house. That's what you want, isn't it? To preserve the house? I swear, it has nothing to do with the rest."

"That's what you *say*, but next time it will be something more," she said. "You've manipulated me for the last time, Jules Danner. Now, if you will please go, I'd like to get back to the shop."

She watched the proud line of Jules's back as he walked away, in the sudden bitter knowledge that to win his point he'd needed to do no more than seize her in his arms and let his mouth once more claim hers. She was powerless to resist him, whatever his demand, if he'd only known. But he hadn't.

Or, perhaps he had. Perhaps such intimacy with her was now distasteful to him. She choked back a sob that rose in her throat.

Chapter Eight

Shaken though she was by this new understanding of herself, Sabrina carried on. She was completing a transaction with the shop's lone customer a short time later when Rhonda Bartlett pushed her way into the store as Jules had predicted. Excusing herself and nodding to Ethel to take over, Sabrina made a broken-field rush through the maze of antiques and came up directly in the path of the decorator, effectively blocking her way to the corner alcove and the tambour desk.

"If you're here about the desk—," began Sabrina.

"Of course I'm here about the desk, darling. I talked with your helper when you were away having your lunch, but you're the person I really came to see."

Across the store from the front door where she had just seen Sabrina's customer on her way, Ethel called out, "I told her you'd sell your full set of god-given teeth before you'd sell that desk, Sabrina."

Ms. Bartlett moved her head to dart a killing glance at Ethel, then back to Sabrina with the plastic smile. She said, "When I saw you out there at Jules's mansion the other day, I could understand your sentimental attachment for your desk," she said in a syrupy voice that Sabrina listened to warily. "Of course you can't bear to think of selling that precious desk to just anyone. Well, I came to set your mind at rest. This client I'm buying it for—"

"How can I make you understand that the desk is not for sale?" Sabrina asked desperately, feeling as if she were drowning in a sea of words. She might as well have been mute.

Ms. Bartlett's words rolled on. ". . . three story townhouse . . . veritable museum . . . atmosphere of charm and grace." The tone was suddenly wheedling. "Now, darling, don't you think it's just a wee bit selfish of you to hide that beautiful piece away in a musty little corner when it could be enjoyed by the very best people—"

"Ms. Bartlett, *please* go," Sabrina interrupted wearily.

All semblance of affability left the decorator's face. "You upstate shopkeepers don't seem to understand that we decorators are your bread and butter," she shrilled. "But don't think you've got Jules tied down with your petty order. You may have aced me out of a commission for the moment, but in the end Jules Danner gets what he wants. When he does, I'll be the one who calls the shots at your precious Glenhaven, don't forget."

"Well, of all the nerve," sputtered Ethel at the back of the store as the woman stalked out.

134

Seething inside, Sabrina was too choked up to speak. "Later Ethel. Not now," she managed to say as she made for her private retreat behind the screen. There she sat with her head in her hands, elbows propped on the disputed desk. The emotion that boiled within her was far deeper and more devastating than mere indignation.

The odious decorator had just confirmed the ugly truth she had suspected from the first but had expelled from her mind. The new mistress of Glenhaven would be Rhonda Bartlett. It was a fact Sabrina must learn to live with. At the same time, her opinion of Jules Danner—that same Jules Danner who, in spite of a commitment to this woman had made ardent advances to her—plummeted to a new low.

"Men!" she muttered disdainfully.

"You say something, Sabrina?" Ethel asked from the other side of the Chinese screen.

At the end of the wretched afternoon when she was about to close shop, Sabrina had one more phone call. It was Ralph. He had to talk to her now, he said, a note of urgency in his voice. It was something that wouldn't wait until Friday.

Where a few days earlier Sabrina would have welcomed this opportunity to tell Ralph once and for all that she was not going to marry him, suddenly, thanks to her night of euphoria followed by a losing day at the hands of Jules Danner, the question of marrying Ralph was open again.

Not that she'd felt any sudden romantic thrill when she heard his voice. To the contrary, the very fact she *hadn't* had all at once seemed very appealing to her.

She'd had her fill of hot chills and heart murmurs, was sick of riding the crest of a golden swell one moment and awash in its fall the next. After what the cunning and mercurial Jules Danner had put her through in the past twenty-four hours, steady, methodical, plan-ahead Ralph looked better, somehow.

While she was quite in tune with the new freedom many women sought and found in this new age, Sabrina knew that for herself it would never be enough. She loved her work—the people, the mystique of antiques, the challenge of tracking them down; the independence of running her own small business—but she had always known, too, that her life would never be complete if she had to live it out alone like Aunt Hat. Marrying Ralph wasn't the worst thing she could do, she told herself bleakly. Heaven only knew what kind of misery she could bring down on her head if she kept on looking for bell ringers.

The usually cheerful living room, which had been her haven of enchantment the night before, seemed dreary and uninviting to Sabrina as she ushered Ralph in that rainy early evening. She had forgotten during the day to lay a fire as was her usual practice. The cable-operated wood lift, filled in the basement and reeled up by her chore boy, was empty. He'd forgotten to fill it again.

Seated across the cold hearth from Sabrina, Ralph wasted nothing on preliminaries. The company, he said, preferred their young executives married. They had done him the honor of elevating him to one of the firm's vice-presidencies; and he, in turn, was ready to give up his bachelorhood. Since she possessed the qualities a man in his position required in a mate, he was asking her to marry him.

Suddenly Sabrina was back on the fence again. Maybe Jules was right. Maybe she *did* blow hot and cold. "I can't give you an answer this minute, Ralph," she said reluctantly.

"Why not?" he asked in surprise. "You must have known what I was leading up to."

"I can't rush into a thing like this."

Ralph was impatient. "I'd hardly call it rushing. We've been seeing each other long enough. You'd think by now you'd know your own mind."

"Maybe I do. I suppose I'm inclined to say yes," Sabrina confessed, a shade annoyed. She added firmly, "I'll tell you this, Ralph, if you're pushing for an answer this minute, the answer is definitely no."

"All right. I won't press you now, but I don't understand you, Sabrina," he said petulantly, clearly dissatisfied but unwilling to risk the finality implied in the promise of an immediate no. "Could you just get on with it, though. The company—well, when I got the promotion they asked me straight out about marriage, and I—well, it never occurred to me that you—"

Sabrina heard no more. A great sense of relief settled upon her. She knew at last for certain that it would never work. Being married to Ralph might be better than going through life with no one; but the thought of marrying both Ralph and The Company made Aunt Hat's aloneness look—well, not *good*, but almost not *bad*.

She was framing the words to tell him when across the room the telephone suddenly rang. "Excuse me," she said instead. She got up and went to the window seat to pick up the phone, Ralph following.

"I'll be on my way. Let me know when you make up your mind," he said, as if they had been discussing a business matter. He gave her a peck on a cheek.

"Wait Ralph. Whoever it is, I'll cut it short," she said hastily. "I really want to talk to you now."

He was already halfway across the living room on his way out. "Go on with your call. I'm in a hurry. I'll expect to hear from you in a day or two."

Sabrina looked after him with a feeling of frustration. She wanted to get the matter over tonight, but she couldn't bring herself to walk away from the phone that pealed insistently beside her hand and go after him. With a sigh, she picked up the phone.

"Sabrina?"

"Aunt Hat! Where in the world are you?"

"Honolulu. We have a stopover here," her aunt's voice came through to her from halfway around the world.

"I can't wait to see you. When will you be home?"

"We've just talked to my friend's son. He expects to drop me off in Sutton late Wednesday afternoon. Look for me then."

"Oh Aunt Hat, you don't know how good it is to hear your voice," said Sabrina, her own voice choked with sudden emotion. "I need you. I'll be so glad to have you home."

By six o'clock Wednesday afternoon, Sabrina's impatience knew no bounds. Her aunt's rooms were ready and waiting, fresh flowers on her coffee table, a fire laid in her small fireplace to be lighted when she arrived.

Hero's bright coat had been brushed by Sabrina to a fine luster. As if the animal knew something special was in the air, he unexpectedly abandoned the invalid role and three-legged hop and bravely ventured to touch ground with the tender foot.

Upstairs in the family living room a fire already blazed cheerfully. Sabrina, in the window seat across the room, kept a restless watch on the street below where the long shadows of the late autumn afternoon had dissolved into gathering dusk. While it was still light enough to see clearly, a silver Rolls-Royce rounded the corner at the cross street two blocks away and moved sedately toward her own driveway where it turned in. From her window seat above, Sabrina caught a glimpse of her aunt's face peering eagerly from the back seat at the house.

She had hardly expected such a posh arrival. She watched curiously for an instant before she came to her senses and flew downstairs to greet the returning traveler. By the time she burst through the door, her aunt was already out of the car and hurrying up the driveway to meet her—a taller-than-average, full-figured woman who even in haste carried herself with grace and dignity. There was a special something about her aunt today that was new and puzzling to Sabrina. Whatever it was, the trip had done the dear soul a world of good, she thought as she opened her arms and the two came together in a warm embrace.

"So good to have you back," she murmured joyfully, burying her head in the soft, ample curve of her aunt's shoulder where she'd found comfort whenever she needed it most of her life. She hugged the big woman with fierce affection for a moment and then stepped off to take a really good look at her and realized for the first time that her aunt, with her crown of white hair and dark eyes, was a striking woman. There was an aura of contentment and well-being about her that Sabrina had never seen before.

"You look marvelous," Sabrina cried with delight.

"And so do you, dear child," her aunt replied, but the shrewd brown eyes continued to examine the niece closely. In the next breath she said, "You're a little thin and shouldn't have those shadows around your eyes. You've either been partying or worrying a lot."

"Partying, of course, darling! You know what a great jet-setter I am," Sabrina said lightly, but even to her own ears her laugh had a hollow ring. She stood pinned for another moment by the pair of concerned eyes until her aunt turned away from her, still keeping an affectionate hold on Sabrina's hand. For the first time Sabrina remembered she and her aunt were not alone.

"Oh, mercy! I quite forgot!" Aunt Harriet exclaimed with a flustered laugh.

Sabrina at last became completely aware of her aunt's friend who stood a few steps away, watching the reunion with a smile. Turning to acknowledge the presence, Sabrina was caught completely off balance to find, not a plump, middle-aged little woman she had pictured in her mind, but a man, a tall, distinguished looking gentleman of about her aunt's age. Overwhelmed though she was, Sabrina had an uncanny feeling that she remembered him from some other place and time.

Even in the throes of her astonishment, she was warmed by a new, wishful pleasure for her aunt in this unexpected turn of events. She turned curiously to size up the son, who was down the driveway, hidden by the trunk of the car where he sorted out her aunt's luggage.

"What a rattlebrain I've turned into," her aunt said, laughing. "You don't remember Archie, of course."

The words fell upon Sabrina's ears at the same moment the son appeared from around the car, and she saw he was Jules Danner. Her senses reeled. He came up the driveway toward the steps where they stood, his arms full of suitcases, a garment carrier, an oversize shopping bag.

Never in her life had Sabrina fainted, but for a second she thought she might. Dimly she heard her aunt's voice carrying on a proper, drawing-room introduction as if it were the most natural thing in the world.

"This is an old friend from years ago, Archibald Danner, dear, and Archie, this is the fine young woman our little Sabrina grew up to be."

As if from a great distance Sabrina heard Archibald Danner say, "You may find this hard to believe, my dear, but when you were very young you took many a ride on my knee."

This can't be happening! Sabrina thought; surely she was losing her mind. As the implications of the scene fell into place, she almost wished she were and her aunt's "friend" were a mere figment of her imagination and not the scoundrel she knew him to be. How could Aunt Harriet forget what this man had done to her own brother? How could she call Archibald Danner her *friend?* she protested inwardly as Jules came up the driveway toward them, moving with his usual sinewy, masculine grace under the load of bags. One glance at his face told her that he had taken stock of the stituation and was enjoying a certain arrogant satisfaction at her expense.

"I believe you know Jules," her aunt said. Sabrina, who had not found her voice since the first shock of revelation, could only nod mutely.

"And how's the Princess?" Jules greeted her with his sardonic smile. She longed to frame a scathing retort, but she held her peace. After a moment of uncomfortable silence, Aunt Hat jumped into the breech.

"Come, come! Are we going to stand out here in the driveway all night?" she asked with false heartiness. "Sabrina, dear, will you lead the way?"

At last Sabrina found her voice to say shakily, "Yes of course, Aunt Hat."

Inside the entrance hall they were met by Hero. The golden retriever came limping sedately down the hallway from the open kitchen door to rub his great head against Jules's knee.

"Ah, the ailing canine," said Jules dryly. "Glad to see he's recovered his aplomb."

Sabrina, without comment, led the way on down the hall and through the French doors that opened into Aunt Harriet's quarters. Danner followed with the luggage; behind him in procession Aunt Hat, his father and the red-gold dog.

"I see there's a fire laid," remarked Jules when he had deposited the bags where their owner indicated. He swept the charming room with a cool glance of approval. "Shall I light it for you, Aunt Harriet?"

Aunt Harriet? Aunt Harriet, indeed! Something within Sabrina cried out in silent protest. Since when had Jules Danner become so intimate with her aunt? Her indignation changed to bewilderment when she heard a note of fond approval in her aunt's voice as she accepted his offer to light the fire.

Somehow Sabrina could not bring herself to walk over and join the threesome assembled companionably across the room. She lingered near the door, watching Jules rearrange the wood for a better draft and touch it with a lighted match. He gave to the ordinary household chore the same panache she'd seen in whatever he undertook. She resented it furiously now. Why did the man do the simplest thing with that easy economy of motion that awakened in her such a painful, unwelcome yearning?

Standing across the small room from the trio gathered in a cozy half-circle before the blazing fire, Sabrina felt shut off from the aunt who had been her polestar from as far back as she could remember. There was a camaraderie about the three of them there in the firelight's glow that did not extend to her.

From her spot near the hearth between father and son, Aunt Hat said, "Come join us, dear. Tell me what you've been up to while I've been away."

Sabrina saw that the two men awaited her answer, the elder with a look only of polite interest; but in the younger man's eyes she saw a cool amusement. She made no move toward the fire.

Then, to her utter astonishment, she heard herself say in answer to her aunt's question, "Well, for one thing, I've been getting engaged."

The reaction across the room was dramatic. It was as if a dark veil had fallen across Jules Danner's face. Her aunt's eyes widened in surprise.

"How exciting," she said. "Anyone I know?"

"Ralph Spurling," Sabrina informed her weakly,

143

considerably dazed by the words she'd just heard from her own mouth. "You've met him."

"I remember. Isn't he that insurance salesman?" asked her aunt.

"Broker," Sabrina dutifully corrected. "He's just been made vice-president of his company."

"Come dad," Jules broke in abruptly, his voice warm with respectful affection, though winter lay deep in his eyes. "Let's get out and give the lady a chance to settle in. It appears she and her niece have some catching-up to do."

In the act of casting Jules a quick look of gratitude for bringing the ordeal to an end, Sabrina caught the cynical glance tossed her way and the significance of his deliberate reference to "catching-up." She bristled. *Let him think she blew hot and cold,* she thought and returned his look with a frosty glare.

"So, what about this engagement, Sabrina?" Aunt Hat asked, eyeing her niece shrewdly when the two men were gone.

"It's really not so much an engagement," Sabrina admitted. "It's just that last night he asked me to marry him." Under her aunt's clinical eye, she was unhappily aware of a rush of color to her face.

"I remember the young man now, quite well. I never dreamed you could be serious about him," her aunt said in a troubled tone. "I always imagined your man would be someone quite different."

"Different? In what way?"

"Someone more like Jules, I should think," her aunt said. "And speaking of Jules, there is something I want to talk to you about, but I'm afraid I'm too tired to go into it tonight."

It was a remark that normally would have aroused Sabrina's curiosity, but not tonight. She could guess what it led to, and she was not yet ready to hear an apologia for her aunt's friendship with her father's betrayer. Conversation lagged after that. There was a constraint between the two women, mercifully broken when Sabrina withdrew to the kitchen to serve the homecoming dinner she had prepared.

Her aunt came to the table bearing gifts and these, along with the bottle of champagne Sabrina popped for the occasion, brought a brief respite from tensions that seemed almost to crackle, like static in the air. The exquisite pieces of jade her aunt had brought her from the far east were so breathtakingly beautiful Sabrina could almost forget for awhile the sorrow and disappointment that lay heavy on her heart; but the balm brought by the jade and champagne was short-lived. At the table the women spoke only of surface things, and Sabrina felt a guilty sense of relief when her aunt pleaded jet lag and took herself off to bed at an early hour.

In the solitude of her own room, Sabrina could find no peace. How could her aunt have a friendly relationship with the unprincipled man who had destroyed Harrison Burke? she asked herself again and again in her wide-awake searching in the insomniac hours of the night; but a still, small voice inside kept reminding her, *What about you, Sabrina Burke? Is your case so different? What about Jules Danner? What about you?*

Dear Aunt Hat, she thought, her heart filled with

shame. There had been no room in her aunt's young life for romance. She had sacrificed whatever personal yearnings she had to care for a widowed and ailing sister-in-law and half-orphaned child. From her own modest inheritance, she had built up a business that could support mother and daughter in later years and give them financial freedom with no further help from her.

Who could blame her? And who knew better than Sabrina the lethal force of the Danner charm? Alone there in the dark, though there was no one to hear her, Sabrina said aloud, "Do what you like, Aunt Hat. You deserve it. Whatever you do is all right."

Chapter Nine

Sabrina awakened the next morning with the sinking realization that her last hope of learning the full story of the Burke-Danner partnership was gone. How could she question her aunt now about Archibald Danner's bad faith? She couldn't, of course. No more could she reconcile herself to the possibility that she might be forced to live out her life without ever learning the true circumstances surrounding her family's tragedy.

Her aunt was still sleeping when she crossed the hallway to the store, feeling worn out and depressed. The arrival of Ethel a few minutes before nine did nothing to raise her spirits.

"I know it's none of my business, Sabrina, but don't you think you've been staying out late too much?" asked Ethel, with a searching look. "I sure hope what you've been doing's fun. You wouldn't know from your face."

"Aunt Hat came home last night. I didn't get much sleep," Sabrina said truthfully, with a wan smile. "Don't worry. I'm fine. I've just been doing some extra work around the house after hours to get it ready for her coming. I suppose I'm a little tired."

She could tell from the doubting look in her employee's eyes that Ethel wasn't buying it, but she hardly noticed, for a way out of her impasse had suddenly occurred to her. Uncle George Channing had always been the family attorney. He would know what happened. Why hadn't she thought of him before?

"I have to go out for awhile," she said to Ethel after she had checked with his law office and found the old gentleman in and free to see her. "You'd better get Dora to help out in the store. I'm not sure how long I'll be gone."

The usual affectionate courtesies observed, George Channing asked on a note of resigned patience, "All right, Sabrina. What's on your mind now?"

"My aunt came back from her trip last night. Archibald Danner brought her home," Sabrina said grimly. "From the looks of things it's not just a casual friendship."

"I get the impression you don't have much use for anyone named Danner, Sabrina," the old man said dryly. "What reprehensible thing has Archie Danner done?"

"That's what I want you to tell me, Uncle George," she cried out pleadingly. "I don't really know. Nobody ever told me anything. I can only guess. Lately I've picked up bits and pieces wherever I could and put them together like a Chinese puzzle."

148

"So that's what you've done? What in sam hill have you come up with?"

"Not enough. I know my father died a pauper, and it's plain to see that Archibald Danner came out of the debacle rich," said Sabrina bitterly. "It's easy enough to draw some conclusions from that."

"Easy enough, but conclusions arrived at by such means aren't necessarily correct," the attorney said severely. "Drat those two well-meaning women! What a mess of trouble they've caused by keeping you in the dark."

"I'm so mixed up, Uncle George," Sabrina said, almost in tears. "I've got to find out what happened. You're the only person I can ask."

"By all means, you should know, my dear." He reached out and patted her hand comfortingly. "You should, and you shall. It's high time somebody broke this conspiracy of silence, and it looks like it's up to me."

There was a long pause while the old attorney seemed to rally his thoughts for a beginning. "Well, in the first place," he said at last, "Archie Danner introduced your parents to each other. The Danners and Glendons were longtime friends, and when Archie brought Harrison up with him from Princeton one Christmas and introduced him to your mother, it turned into the love affair of the year."

The old man's beginning words were reassuring to Sabrina. It pleased her to hear that her parents' romance was the kind she dreamed of for herself; but her pleasure was short-lived as the tone of the disclosures began to shift.

Her father, it seemed, was the last of three generations to spend the fortune amassed by his great-grandfather Burke. A charming, scholarly man, he had no business sense; and there was little Burke money left, outside of his sister Harriet's separate small inheritance from the great-grandfather. According to the old attorney, the aging Glendon welcomed his son-in-law into the company, but Sabrina's father never really understood the shipping business; and when her Grandfather Glendon died, leaving the company in her father's hands, he ran it with great style but no common sense, losing large sums of money in a variety of impractical ventures until, when the company was on the verge of collapse, he called upon his old friend Archie Danner to come to the rescue. "Danner was a good businessman who had done well with his own interests," said Uncle George. "He came out of friendship, investing a considerable sum of his own money in the shipping firm. Thus, the Burke-Danner partnership was formed, and Danner gradually steered the flagging business back on the track. Things were going well for the partnership. Then Archibald Danner's wife died."

"Go on, Uncle George," Sabrina urged in a choked voice when the old lawyer came to a halt and lapsed into a long silence. Channing shook his head.

"Well, I don't know about this, Sabrina," he said. "Your mother grew up with Archie Danner and loved him like a brother. Being a kind, sympathetic woman, she went out of her way to lavish attention on the bereaved man, and as near as I can figure Harry just took it wrong. He got the crazy idea there was something going on between those two, and he came to me to have the partnership dissolved. Said Archie was trying to steal his wife, which wasn't the case at all."

Overcome with the enormity of what she had heard, Sabrina gazed in mute anguish at her aged friend. At last she said dully, "And I supposed it was over money."

"Well it wasn't," Uncle Geroge told her bluntly. "Archie wouldn't even take his own funds when he left. He knew very well if he did the company would collapse."

"In spite of that, the company *did* collapse." Her words were hardly more than a bleak whisper.

"Two years later. Luckily, Archie made his other investments with his head instead of his heart so he was able to recover in time." The old gentleman rose ponderously to his feet to signify he had said all he was going to say. Sabrina bade him a dazed good-bye.

In a state of near shock she left him, too preoccupied with her own painful thoughts to go back to the store under Ethel's curious eyes or home to face Aunt Hat. She turned instead to the river, heedless of Jules's warning that she should not walk there alone; though at first she took the precaution of staying on the more frequented paths. Wrapped in her own dark thoughts, she was lost to the morning's misty beauty and, in time, wandered unthinking off the well-traveled pathway onto an unkempt woodland trail.

A few steps along the way she was brought suddenly, terrifyingly to her senses by a strong arm which seized her from behind, pinning her own arms defenselessly to her sides while a hand pressed over her mouth to muffle her cry of alarm. There she was held, paralyzed with fright, for perhaps the count of five. As suddenly as she was grabbed she was released.

"For heaven's sake, Sabrina, you've got to be the

most pigheaded woman alive!" It was Jules Danner's voice. She turned to face him, and her momentary relief turned to rage.

"Of all the rotten tricks!" she cried shakily. "What do you mean, scaring me out of my wits?"

"I thought I told you never to walk down here alone!" The velvet baritone was harsh with a rage of its own. "Somebody's got to scare some sense into you. I rather doubt that your insurance salesman has the good sense to keep you on a leash."

Stung by the arrogant thrust, Sabrina snapped, "Leave Ralph out of this. Since you're so keen about leashes, why don't you put that decorator of yours on one? And may I remind you, what I do with my life is my business. It's hardly a concern of yours."

A look of fury and frustration flashed in the dark eyes and for a moment she wondered if he were about to strike her. He pulled her into his arms, instead, and gave her a hard, brutal kiss. He pushed her away from him, leaving her lips bruised and tingling.

"You're right! Get yourself attacked and robbed! Marry Ralph Spurling. What you do with yourself is no concern of mine. I certainly will stay out of your affairs." He turned and strode away from her up the path, his state of mind eloquently expressed in the angry thrust of the broad shoulders and head. Watching him go, all her anger washed away in a flood of hot tears.

"Jules," she called after him.

"Go to the devil!" he called back savagely, from between tight lips.

"Jules!" She cried it louder this time, cried out on a

note of despair. He kept going. He disappeared over the embankment. He did not look back.

Her heart heavy, Sabrina followed up the trail to the pathway and so on home, wondering miserably why she had quarreled with Jules again now that her doubts about him and his father had been stilled. In the final analysis, she had never been wronged by Jules. He had a perfect right to marry Rhonda Bartlett and do what he liked with Glenhaven. So what were they quarreling about?

At home she found her aunt in the kitchen setting the table for their lunch. From the oven the fragrance of Sabrina's favorite quiche sifted out on the air.

"I think I mentioned last night I have something to talk to you about, Sabrina," said her aunt after their initial greeting. "I'm sure you won't want to continue this nonsense of the restraining order I overheard Jules speak of to his father when you hear what I have to say."

Sabrina's eyes widened in consternation. "Oh, dear lord! The restraining order!" she murmured. "Excuse me, Aunt Hat." She left the kitchen and hurried across the hall to the shop where she dialed the number of George Channing's office.

"You caught me as I was going out the door, Sabrina," the old lawyer told her. "What's it about now?"

"It's that restraining order, Uncle George. I forgot all about it this morning. Would you withdraw it, please."

"That's a good girl. Jules isn't going to do anything bad to the old house."

"I hope you're right," Sabrina said doubtfully. "But whether or not you are, he can festoon it with gargoyles or paint the rooms black, as you said. It's his."

"I guess the order can wait a day or so, can't it? I'm just taking off on a little outing with one of my grandsons. He's waiting double-parked out in front of my office now."

"We-ell, could you get someone there at your office to at least arrange it so Jules can send workmen out to clear away the underbrush?" Sabrina demurred. "He's terribly concerned—"

At the other end of the line Channing cleared his throat. After a pause, he said, "Well, you might as well know, I already took care of that for Jules, after you turned him down and he came to me, and he told me you had it in for him and why. For obvious reasons, he didn't feel he was the one to tell you the truth, you can understand that, so I took it upon myself to change the restraining order. I figured the worst you could do is have me disbarred, and that doesn't scare me much at my age."

Sabrina drew a great sigh. "Thank you, Uncle George, for all you've done. I'm sorry to have been so much trouble."

"It's all right, honey. It's not your fault, you didn't know what you were doing." At least Uncle George wasn't mad at her anymore, she thought wryly as she hung up in the warmth of the old gentleman's approval.

"What's the matter with you, Sabrina? You look like you've seen a ghost," her aunt said when she came back to the kitchen.

"In a way maybe I have," Sabrina admitted unhappily. "I've been to see Uncle George Channing. He told me what happened between my father and Mr. Danner."

Her aunt voiced a small groan. "That's what I was going to talk to you about. Jules told me you had it all wrong," she said sadly. "I should have told you long ago, but it wasn't easy. It was a terrible time for us all. I'll never forget Archie's face when he came to say good-bye to your mother and me."

"My mother never forgave my father, did she?"

"Oh no. She forgave him. She could forgive him anything, she adored him so. He never forgave himself."

"Then why was my mother bitter? Why did we dodge any subject that had to do with my father? I got so I was afraid to ask," said Sabrina reproachfully.

A look of distress fell upon her aunt's face. "Oh dear. George Channing didn't tell you all," her aunt said. After a moment of brooding silence, she went on. "Your father was a proud, sensitive man, Sabrina, too proud to admit he was wrong about Archie. At the same time, he couldn't live with the thought of what he had done to his friend. That and the fact he couldn't make a go of the company by himself filled the poor man with self-contempt. He began to drink himself into forgetfulness at night, and on top of that took sleeping pills. One night, after too many martinis he took too many pills."

"But you told me he died of a heart attack!" said Sabrina, overcome with the enormity of what she'd just heard.

"No. I said, 'heart trouble'—more accurately, a broken heart. Your mother lost her will to live then and was in failing health for the rest of her life. She died of a blood disease fifteen years later, but you might say she too died of a broken heart."

As luck would have it, there was a steady stream of customers in and out all afternoon. Sabrina, locked in her own tormented thoughts, dealt with them absently as they came and went. She somehow got through the rest of the day under Ethel's frankly curious scrutiny. Alone with her aunt before the upstairs fireplace in the early evening, the emotions she had kept dammed up for so many hours at last flooded over.

"Oh, Aunt Hat, I've made such a mess of things," she moaned. "If I'd only known a month ago what I've found out today!"

"Dear girl, stop flogging yourself. It's no fault of yours. The fault is mine. You should have been told. It was just easier to put it from the mind," her aunt told her. "No great harm's been done, I'm sure."

"If you only knew—" But she couldn't go on. She sat staring moodily into the fire, absorbed with her own unhappy thoughts.

Her aunt broke into them presently. "One thing I don't understand, if you'll pardon my asking. It's about Jules. I remember him as a wonderful youngster who was your particular champion when you were a very small girl. I was quite taken by him on the drive up from the city yesterday. What has he done to make you dislike him so?"

"*Dislike him!*" cried Sabrina. "I don't dislike him,

Aunt Hat, though I'll admit, I tried to hard enough. It just didn't work. When Uncle George told me all those things about my father today—" She shuddered, and her words came to an abrupt halt. Her aunt watched anxiously. After a moment Sabrina, with great reluctance, went on. "That first moment when I really understood what had happened back then, I confess my first feeling was relief."

"Relief?" her aunt repeated, plainly mystified.

"Oh not that I wasn't terribly sorry and sad, of course; but at the same time I was relieved to know at last that it wasn't my duty to hate the Danners," she said. "Knowing that, I could live with the rest."

"But why did you feel obliged to include Jules in your hostility?" her aunt asked. "Archie I can understand, in view of what you thought was the truth, but Jules was still in his teens when it all happened. You couldn't think he had any part in it."

"It seemed reasonable that he got his business start on money his father had taken from mine. Besides, oh, Aunt Hat, every time I've had anything to do with him I've come away feeling such a fool. I can't tell you how . . ." As if a floodgate had been let open, with a great sense of release, Sabrina found herself pouring out all the pain and frustrations of her various encounters with Jules Danner, slowly at first and then with gathering momentum until she was dredging up even half-remembered moments that had slipped her mind before.

As she unburdened herself, a new and shameful suspicion crept into her mind. Hadn't she really meant to punish Jules all along; punish him because he planned to make Rhonda Bartlett the new mistress at Glenhaven—more painful still—his wife? Hadn't she seized upon the newspaper article, which left so much to her vengeful imagination as an instrument to discredit him in her own eyes?

"Oh, Aunt Harriet," she cried when the full import of her actions struck her. "How could I be such a spiteful person? How could Jules ever forgive me for what I have done?"

Her aunt studied the beautiful, emotion-wracked face of her niece closely. Her voice was full of loving compassion when she replied, "Dear Sabrina, child, all you've done is to act like a woman in love."

Her words freed Sabrina suddenly to accept the splendid, unhappy truth that she had understood deep down inside almost from the first. "You're right, Aunt Harriet. I am in love with Jules," she said quietly after a moment of thought, scarcely aware of the tears that spilled down her face. Her aunt saw them and moved over to Sabrina's chair and took the young woman in her arms. From a pocket she took a soft linen handkerchief and wiped the tears away as she had when her niece was a child.

"Silly girl," she chided gently. "Love is a wonderful thing."

"Not when it's hopeless, Aunt Harriet. Jules plans to marry someone else," Sabrina told her sorrowfully. "But that doesn't really have anything to do with the fact that he abhors the sight of my face after all I've done."

"I'm sure you are wrong."

"I wish I were. I saw him this morning. He made it all too clear how he feels."

Sabrina took particular pains when she dressed the next morning to cover up the clear evidence her face bore of yet another sleepless night. Hoping to avoid Ethel's inevitable "You all right, Sabrina?," she brushed on a rosy "blusher" with a generous hand and slipped into a soft wool dress which, though old, was a flattering shade of ashes-of-roses that made her appear more vibrantly healthy than she felt.

She'd made such a hopeless mess of her personal life there was no hope of changing it. The least she could do was put on a cheerful face and not inflict her own dissatisfactions on the rest of her world. She crossed the hall and entered the store, determined to focus all her attention on her business from now on and close the doors of her mind to such painful distractions as family sorrows long past and beyond repair and the all-too-present ache in her heart for a love that would never be consummated.

No longer dared she let her mind hark back to her moments of awakening—the touch of his hands, his lips; his body so hard against hers it sent a spear of fire cutting through to her very depths. The pain of loss such maundering aroused was too great to be born.

It was a busy morning at the store. Between customers she plugged away doggedly at the tambour desk on the store's account books. She greeted all comers with a determinedly cheerful smile.

Late in the morning came a telephone call from Ralph. It must be Friday, she thought guiltily when she heard his voice. With all the disturbing elements of the past forty-eight hours, she had quite forgotten about Ralph. She should have gotten in touch with him and given the final no she intended to.

"I thought I'd hear from you before this," he said reproachfully. "I've been wondering if you'd made up your mind."

"Well—yes. I suppose I have," she replied after a moment of hesitation, tempted all at once to give him her rejection over the phone. It would be much easier than having to face him with it, she thought, yet she somehow couldn't bring herself to dispose of such a serious matter as a marriage proposal with a few words poured into a telephone. Busy with her own ethical considerations, it was a moment before Sabrina brought her attention back to Ralph's voice still on the line.

"In that case," he was saying, "I'll pick you up early for dinner this evening—about, oh, say a little before six." Before she fully realized he had put a wrong interpretation on her words and took the matter to be settled in the affirmative, he said a word in parting and hung up.

She stared at the dead phone in her hand, appalled at the situation as it now appeared. It was, of course, out of the question to let him go into the evening like this with false hope, yet the only alternative was to call him back. In spite of her strong feelings against demeaning one of the most important questions a man could ask by disposing of it in such a casual fashion, she would have to give her answer over the phone.

To her dismay, she found when she reached Ralph's office that he had not made the call from there. His secretary had no idea where he might be reached for the rest of the morning.

"What about this afternoon?" asked Sabrina.

"I'm sorry," the secretary said, "Mr. Spurling will be in conference all afternoon."

Sabrina hung up and buried her face in her hands. What a mess! she thought. Now she would have to struggle through a last, uneasy dinner with Ralph, knowing all the time that at its end she would give him an answer he wasn't prepared to hear; unless, of course, she told him what she had to say at the moment he came to pick her up. There would be no dinner to endure after that. She would be permanently stricken from that Master Plan—and high time, she thought.

It was a tidy solution, had it worked. As it turned out, when Ralph did arrive that early evening, and Sabrina came down to answer the door, she found to her consternation that he had come straight from the office and had a man with him outside in the car.

"Come on. Where's your coat?" Ralph said, in a hurry. "I've got this fellow from the office waiting outside. He left his car at a station this morning to be serviced. Since it's on our way, I gave him a ride. Go get your coat."

There would be no opportunity now to discuss anything before dinner, she realized as she went back upstairs to get her coat. She put her head in Aunt Hat's door to tell her, with a helpless shrug, that she was going out after all and would see her when she returned.

"Might as well fill the tank as long as I'm here," Ralph said as they reached the station where they were to drop off his passenger. He pulled up to the gas pumps, and when the attendant ambled over to take care of his customer, Ralph told him to fill the tank and check everything. That taken care of, the two men got out; Ralph to make sure he was given full service; the other to go on his way.

Sabrina, waiting in the car, felt her pulse do a quick two-step and race on in double time as her eyes caught a glimpse of a cream-colored Mercedes in the passing stream of traffic. The driver maneuvered expertly through the line of cars and swung unexpectedly into the gas station and up to a bank of pumps across from where she sat. She didn't have to look a second time to know that it was Jules Danner at the wheel.

She prayed to be made invisible. After yesterday's traumatic encounter, she wasn't prepared to face Jules with his deeply probing eyes; but her desperate hope that he wouldn't notice her where she sat was soon dashed. Jules stepped out of the Mercedes and after a brief instruction to the attendant, turned at once and walked directly across the paved strip between the two banks of pumps to Ralph's car.

Sabrina, suddenly shameless, watched him come with a fullness in her heart so great she could scarcely breathe. Her whole being cried to reach out to him, but only their eyes met. For an instant she felt it might be splendid to drown in the cool, lake-blue depths of his. Then Ralph stepped up, and the thrill of the moment was lost in the sudden grip of alarm.

Jules's brows lifted and his mouth curved in the twist of the sardonic smile she had come to dread.

"Sabrina," he said with a slight formal nod of greeting before turning to offer a hand to Ralph. "May I congratulate you? I understand Sabrina and you are to be married."

"Dear Lord, don't let this be happening," Sabrina cried out silently within. From somewhere beyond her anguish she heard Ralph's voice, pleased and smug.

"Why thanks, Danner," he was saying with surprise. "I didn't think she'd told anyone yet."

"Have I spoken out of turn, Sabrina?" Jules said with terrible innocence. He leaned down to peer through the window at her wickedly. "I just happened to be on the scene when she told her aunt, but don't worry. It will go no further. I wouldn't think of spoiling the fun."

"Well, thanks," said Ralph, still plainly uncertain what to make of it, but looking self-satisfied.

With a farewell lift of his hand, Jules left and went back to tend to his car, leaving Sabrina seething inside—at herself as much as at Jules. In the disturbing aftermath of the recent family disclosures, she had all but forgotten that foolish, impetuous reference to an "engagement" on the night of Aunt Hat's return. Now it had come back on Jules's lips to haunt her. She had only herself to blame. What had possessed her to say such a thing in the first place? she wondered unhappily and recognized it at once for the shameful thing it was—a dart aimed at Jules.

As Ralph drove out of the service station, Sabrina could not resist a side glance toward Jules, now back with his Mercedes, in the act of paying the attendant. She saw him lift his head to look after them and wished for an instant of clairvoyance that she might read the brooding in the ruggedly handsome face as he watched them go.

"Seems to be a good fellow, Danner," said Ralph when they were again back in the stream of traffic.

"Maybe you could be useful in helping me get his insurance business. You'll invite him to the wedding, of course."

Sabrina sucked in her breath and let it out slowly again before she spoke. "There isn't going to be any wedding, Ralph—at least not between you and me," she said evenly. "You'd better take me home. This isn't the way I would have chosen to tell you, believe me, and I'm sorry about that. I really am but the whole thing's gotten out of hand, and it's got to be said now."

"What do you mean, there isn't going to be a wedding?" Ralph said, disbelieving.

"Just that. I'm not going to marry you, Ralph," she said firmly.

"But you said—"

"I said I wanted to think about it. It didn't take me as long as I expected to know the answer was no. You're a good man, Ralph, but I don't love you," she told him. "I wanted to tell you the other night, but the phone rang and you went tearing off. I couldn't get you to wait."

"But Danner said—"

"I know what 'Danner said,' and I'm sorry about that, too," she said miserably. "It was all a mistake. Don't ask me to explain. I'm not even sure I understand how it happened, myself."

"Well, I most certainly don't understand *you*, Sabrina," Ralph said crossly. "First it's yes and now it's no. It looks like I've just been wasting a lot of time."

"Heaven forbid you waste any more. Let's forget about dinner. Just take me home."

He didn't argue. Sabrina rather thought he was relieved. By the time they reached the house and parted company for the last time without the customary kiss, she sensed that Ralph had already made his adjustments and considered himself well out of it. He'd taken her measure again and decided that such an unpredictable woman would not make a suitable wife for a Company Man.

Chapter Ten

Until lately, she had rather imagined she managed her life at least as well as most. Alone, over her coffee next morning—her aunt was still in her room—Sabrina reviewed the shambles she'd managed to make of it the past few weeks and felt thoroughly out of sorts. She had treated Ralph shabbily, for one thing. She had used him as a kind of insurance policy against the kind of future she had envisioned—from the looks of things, prematurely—for Aunt Hat; and though it was evident Ralph had been no more hurt by her than to have his schedule delayed, it was a sorry performance of which she was not proud.

But the true cause of her dissatisfaction this morning had nothing to do with Ralph. The true cause was that she had succeeded in alienating Jules forever, the first man she had ever loved. From the depths of her love, she feared he must surely be the last.

Self-recriminations gouged her like pebbles in a boot as she took up her duties at the store, evading Ethel's inquisitive probings by the simple ploy of retreating to her books behind the screen whenever the two were alone in the store.

It was one of those days when nothing went right. A valuable vase slipped from a customer's hands and shattered upon the floor. The books wouldn't balance. The hourly chorus of clocks, which Sabrina normally looked forward to and paused in her work to enjoy, drove her crazy this morning: reminding her unexplainably of Jules; until she considered putting an end to the assault on her ears by letting them all run down.

By the time Ethel returned from lunch, Sabrina was glad to leave the shop and its sounds for the peace and quiet of her home across the hall.

Instead of going into the kitchen as she usually did, she glanced through the door and seeing that only one place had been set for lunch, she turned down the hall to her aunt's open door where she found Aunt Hat dressed in a stunning red cashmere suit she'd had made in Hong Kong. She was packing an overnight case.

"What's up?" asked Sabrina.

Her aunt looked up from what she was doing, plainly aware for the first time of her niece's presence.

"Oh Sabrina, forgive me for deserting you when I've no more than gotten home," her aunt apologized. "Archie had season tickets to the symphony and Perlman is guest soloist tonight. It's such a long drive back from Manhattan at night, I think I'll stay in town. I hope you don't mind."

"Of course I don't mind. I'm delighted," Sabrina said truthfully. "What about lunch?"

"I've already eaten. Archie will be along any minute," her aunt replied. "There's a nice little chicken pie in the oven for you, dear."

It would be Sabrina's first meeting with Jules's father since she had learned the true story of his relationship with hers, and she felt a moment of panic as the door chime announced his arrival. She tried to recall what she had said and done at their previous meeting, but all she could remember was the deep feeling of resentment against father and son that burned in her that night. The best she could hope for was that in the flurry of that homecoming, her coldness had gone unobserved.

"Answer it, would you please, Sabrina? There's a dear," her aunt called out from her dressing room where she was putting a last touch to her makeup; and though she would have preferred to stay hidden behind the bulwark of her aunt's reassuring person, Sabrina was obliged to go.

She was greatly relieved to be greeted with hearty affection by Archibald Danner. It immediately dispelled her fears. In a few moments they were chatting together like old friends; which, Danner hastened to point out, in truth they were. She was delighted to find the elder Danner as personable as he was distinguished and handsome. In the few minutes it took her aunt to perform her final leave-taking chores, the last vestiges of that old villain had vanished from Sabrina's mind forever, and in his place she found a warm and respected friend.

"Harriet, have you told Sabrina?" Danner asked her aunt when the older woman appeared in the doorway with her overnight case. Aunt Hat stopped short, noticeably flustered. She shook her head.

"Oh, Archie, no," she said in confusion. "The poor darling has had some unhappy things to make adjustments to. It didn't seem an appropriate time."

"Then she's about due for something happy, wouldn't you say? How about telling her now?" asked Danner. After a moment's hesitation her aunt nodded.

"Your Aunt Harriet has agreed to do me the honor of marrying me, Sabrina," Danner announced. "I hope we have your approval, my dear."

"Oh, Aunt Hat!" Sabrina cried, overcome with emotion. She hugged her aunt fiercely, and for a moment forgot her own unhappiness in a burst of happiness for her aunt. Turning then to Danner, she stretched up to give the tall man a hug around the neck and a kiss on the cheek.

"That's one of the nicest things I've heard in weeks," she said softly, seriously. Unexpectedly, she laughed. "I don't mind telling you how considerate of you this is," she said to Danner, twinkling. "I've been standing here wondering what I should call you. 'Mr. Danner' seemed too distant, somehow, and I certainly couldn't say 'Archie.' My aunt didn't bring me up to call her generation by first names. You've solved the problem, and I do thank you, Uncle Archie."

She sent them on their way with love and went back to the store, warmed by the afterglow of happiness shared with them; but as the afternoon shadows grew long, the pleasure she'd felt was chilled by the ghost of her own loneliness; and at last a note of uneasiness crept in. After Aunt Hat and his father were married, would Jules's dislike for her interfere with the close relationship between herself and her aunt? And what about family gatherings? Could she bear to sit at a holiday table across from Rhonda Bartlett and Jules?

The dismal day drew to a close at last. Though she was relieved to have it over and done with, Sabrina took her time about locking up. She dragged her feet at the thought of crossing the hall to her lonely quarters where the only creature awaiting her was the red-gold dog. This night, as she secured the door to the shop behind her, the house she stepped into seemed forlornly empty.

As if somehow he sensed her need for company, the golden retriever waited in the kitchen door to welcome her. He bounded across the hall when she appeared and greeted her with little rumbles of joy deep in his throat. She stopped a moment to scratch his ears and to examine the healing paw he remembered to hold up limply for her to examine, speaking to her in such a pitiful whimper she had to laugh aloud.

"Hero, you clown! You're such a phony. That foot's practically well," she scolded playfully. "Come on now. Let's go and see what I can find to eat."

She foraged in the refrigerator and came up with a bit of ham and a wedge of leftover quiche. These, with a cup of tea and an old-fashioned Baldwin apple from a backyard tree, made her meal. She considered taking it upstairs to eat before the fire but decided she preferred canine company to her own and set a place for herself at the kitchen table.

The retriever curled up on the floor beside her and watched each bite she put in her mouth with such begging eyes she couldn't resist slipping him bits of forbidden food from her plate. When she had finished eating and taken care of her few dishes, Sabrina gave the dog a parting pat and, though she dreaded the feeling of emptiness she knew awaited her in the other part of the house, she crossed the hall and climbed the stairs. The living room seemed gray and cheerless. She stopped only long enough to lay and light a fire before going to her room.

In the bathroom she ran a tubful of hot water, hoping she could thaw the frost that chilled her spirits in a long, luxurious soak, but the tub held no solace for her. She stepped dripping out on the mat, wrapping herself in an oversize towel. Glancing around for her nightgown and finding she'd left it in her room, she dried herself and slipped into the citron silk robe that hung on the dressing room door.

The soft fabric enfolded her nakedness like an embrace. Inside the robe she shivered unexpectedly, and her body undulated in a small involuntary dance. Her mood lifted. She was suddenly exquisitely aware of silk caressing her bare flesh. Languorously she moved on to the living room, buttoning the long row of silk-covered buttons between her breasts, down to the last button below her knees as she went.

Like a cat in the winter sun, Sabrina stretched voluptuously on the deep pile velvet rug, soaking in the warmth from the fire as she watched the flames lick up the flue. Empty-minded, she made no attempt to shut out the image of Jules Danner when it crept in to fill the vacuum but let herself dream that this creature of her imagination was the living, breathing Jules.

So vividly did she realize the image that she fell

under the spell of its overpowering masculine presence as she pictured him there beside her before the fire, as real as if he were there in the flesh.

In her flight of fancy, he fondled her with small kisses and gently exploring hands that grew ever more urgent. Their lips clung together hungrily. His hands burned brands upon her nakedness. Streams of fire spilled through her veins until she imagined herself at last swept along by the hard-driving maleness of the real man, into a rapturous awakening denied her except in dreams. In a final ecstatic transport, she cried out his name aloud, and the sound of her own voice brought her back to reality.

Breathing heavily as if she had just escaped from wild waters, she pulled herself free of the dream. It did not let her go easily. Her mind still teeming with futile wishes, abortive hopes, she slowly, painfully withdrew.

How sweet it might have been—Jules and herself, his father and Aunt Harriet! If only she had known in time that she was fighting windmills of her own making, what a congenial family they might have become. If only, in spite of her own wrong-headedness, Jules could love her and forgive what she had done.

If only . . . If only . . . but when she came to the bottom line—the last insoluble "if only"—there was Rhonda Bartlett. *If only Jules had never chosen another woman to be his wife!*

Her escape into fantasy ended there, leaving her stripped of all material for making daydreams. She must teach herself how to live with the fact she and Jules would never belong to each other. She must face the reality that the only man she could ever love could not love her. When she accepted this as the truth, she was without dreams—without hope—alone.

Though normally a person who welcomed intervals of solitude, there was no enjoyment for Sabrina in being by herself tonight. All her earlier pleasure in the play of firelight and all the delight in the caress of her robe were gone. She stared moodily into the receding flames as loneliness closed in upon her.

After a time, she jumped up and fumbled with bare feet for her discarded slippers, decided on the spur of the moment to violate a long-standing house rule that confined Hero to the downstairs rooms. She padded across the living room to the stairway, bent on bringing the golden retriever up into forbidden territory, not to indulge the animal but to buffer her loneliness.

"So I spoil him!" she said aloud defiantly to the absent Jules. "*He* loves me, and a lot you care."

She had reached the landing at the foot of the stairs when the front doorbell rang. From where she stood she saw through the one-way glass panel at one side of the door the tall, heart-shattering figure of Jules Danner in the light of the driveway; as if, by defying him in his absence, she had conjured him there somehow. Seized with a foolish panic, Sabrina turned to flee.

She had taken only two steps upward in her retreat when a chilling possibility flashed across her mind and arrested her feet. What if his father and Aunt Harriet had been in an accident, what if they had been hurt? The moment she thought the terrible thought she was sure it must be true. What other explanation could there be for Jules's presence out there? Nothing short of a disaster would otherwise bring him here.

Half-sick with apprehension, she turned back down the stairs, stumbling in her haste so she had to grab the banister to keep from falling on the last step. She flew across the lower landing and flung open the door. Across the threshold, Jules moved back a step in astonishment at her unexpected appearance in dishabille.

"What has happened to them? Is she all right?" Sabrina cried, quite unaware of the picture she made in the light from the porch which fell like a spot on the pale citron silk robe and highlighted her flushed cheeks and the damp hair that curled in soft tendrils around her face.

"Is who all right?" asked Jules in a puzzled tone.

"Aunt Hat. Your father. Are they all right?"

"As far as I know, they are. They looked fine the last I saw of them a few hours ago," Jules assured her. "Is there any reason to think they're not?"

A great lump dissolved in Sabrina's throat. "Thank God!" she said softly, too relieved to say more for a moment.

Her alarm stilled, she became at once burningly aware of the man across the threshold—the man, who so short a time ago had been the subject of her yearning fantasies. She dared not speak again until she could control the timbre of her voice, knowing that if she did, she might reveal too much. When she at last found confidence to answer him, it was with no trace of the painful emotions that lay just under the surface of her words.

"Wasn't it you who told me the other day that we had nothing to say to each other," she said. "Naturally, I just assumed it would take a disaster to bring you to my

174

door." To her dismay, as she spoke she realized how hostile her words must sound. This time, she hadn't intended them to be. She was suddenly afraid that if she lingered, she might commit further offense and turned away from him on sudden impulse; knowing only that it wasn't in her heart to quarrel with Jules anymore.

"Oh no you don't," Danner said sternly. In a step he was across the threshold, seizing her by the shoulders, turning her half around to face him. "When will you learn that you can't run away from me, Sabrina?" he asked in a chiding, paternal voice.

While his strong hands held her in their tightening grip she could not raise her eyes to meet his. She struggled to wrench herself free, knowing that the truth of her love for him was there to be read if their eyes should meet.

"Let me go—*please,*" she begged in desperation; but he continued to hold her firmly with one hand and—as on another still unforgotten encounter—he cupped her chin with the other. She let it stay, knowing within her there was no longer any will to resist.

With gentle force he turned her face to his so there was nothing to do but to look in his eyes. Deep and unreadable, they gazed into hers for a long moment before he sighed and shook his head and let her go. The dark eyes continued to search her face. Free now to move, Sabrina stayed where he left her, still under their compelling spell.

"Why, Sabrina? Why?" he asked suddenly, out of the growing silence. "Why do you fight me at every turn? You pretend to hate me, but both of us know you don't, at least right now you don't. Tell me the truth, Sabrina. Was there really ever a time you did?"

Now that she had no more angry answers to Jules's questions, she had no answers at all. Wordless, she stood like a culprit before the bench; eyes downcast, heart beating so wildly she feared he must notice the swift rise and fall of her breast beneath its quilted covering of citron silk.

Again the silence grew between them as Jules waited for her answer. When none was forthcoming, he carried on.

"I could understand all this when you thought your family had been badly used by mine, but your Aunt Harriet says that's been cleared up," he said in a tone of bafflement. "Tell me, Sabrina, what are we fighting for now?"

Reminded again of the willful injustice she had done Jules's good father and, from the day of their first meeting, the foolish hostility she had harbored for Jules, a sorrow of shame swept over Sabrina. Her voice choked with emotion, she looked up at the beloved man before her with stricken eyes. Finding no words to express her remorse, she whispered like an act of contrition, "Jules . . . Jules . . ."

In the next moment she was in his arms, her head cradled upon the firm plane below his collarbone. A strong, gentle hand stroked her hair.

"Never mind," he said quietly, reassuringly, close to her ear. "It's all right. It's time we put all that behind us, anyhow."

He tipped up her chin again to explore her face, not with his eyes this time, but with his lips; brushing her hairline, her forehead, the lobes of her ears; and on to her mouth where their lips met softly and clung, parted and clung again; parted at last, his own moving on to nuzzle her throat and the small, sweet-scented hollow at the base of her neck.

Like wildfire, a shiver raced through Sabrina's body at the touch of Jules's cheek brushing the beginning curve of her breast where the silken robe fell open. She was suddenly acutely conscious of her nakedness beneath the layers of silk and of the two top buttons she had neglected to fasten, giving away her state of undress. She felt a wave of color rush to her face; and at the same instant Jules swept her up in his arms.

All other concerns were lost as she gave herself to the moment. A small voice from some far-off place inside her said she was shameless, that she must pull herself together and prepare to resist this man when they passed the head of the stairs; but she was distracted by a breathless excitement that whispered through her like a summer breeze, and she hardly listened, strangely unable to make herself care what the voice of prudence might have to say.

Through the soft silk of the robe Sabrina was deliciously aware of the play of muscles moving powerfully but with an incredible economy of effort, as Jules carried her up the stairs and across the landing to the living room.

As gravely as a high priest to the altar, he bore her to the fireplace; her heart pounding fiercely, body tingling in unguarded consent. There he set her sedately in the wing chair at the far side of the hearth. Then, while eagerness fluttered like a captive bird in her breast, he left her. Turning away, he went to the far side of the fireplace and, to her surprise and consternation, seated himself on the love seat facing her, a full hearth-length away.

"To get back to the matter that brought me here tonight," he said casually, to her dismay as if nothing unusual had passed between them at the foot of the stairs, "I was notified late this afternoon that you've had a change of heart about the restraining order. I came by to thank you for having it called off."

His words struck Sabrina with the force of a body blow. Of all the ways she could imagine the tender encounter might play itself out, she could never have expected this. So deep was her hurt she felt it as almost a physical pain. Yet clearly enough, to him it had been no more than a passing diversion. What a fool she had been to read meanings where no meanings lay. To the cool, handsome man across the hearth it meant nothing. He was merely here on a courtesy call.

"There's no need to thank me," she said crisply. "I haven't changed my mind in the least about the awful things you expect to do to Glenhaven."

"Are you trying to pick another quarrel with me, Princess?" Jules asked quizzically, plainly amused.

There it was—that hateful name again. *Princess,* indeed! Almost without intending to, Sabrina found herself asking with blunt annoyance, "Why do you call me that, for heaven's sake?"

"Princess? I never really thought about it. Let's see if I can explain." The strong, chiseled face softened in thought, the eyes far away. Sabrina waited, watching with bitterness, still tasting the acrid poison of her recent betrayal; expecting nothing from this man but more betrayal, whatever he had to say.

"That goes back to when I was a kid," Jules continued shortly, the deep blue eyes coming back from some distant time to fix on hers. "There was this baby at

Glenhaven then. Somehow while I wasn't looking it turned into a beautiful young woman—like a butterfly from a chrysalis. From a bundle of blankets, a Princess, no less. That's all there is to it."

A likely tale, thought Sabrina watching him uncertainly for some covert sign of duplicity. It was a pretty story, but could it possibly be true? she wondered. In spite of his cool dismissal of the moments upon the stairs, she wanted all at once to believe. Doubting, but somewhat mollified, she tentatively accepted his explanation at its face value.

"Do what you like with the house," she said in an effort to show she could be agreeable in return. "After all, it's really none of my business."

"Not if you marry Ralph Spurling, it isn't," Jules said, his voice level.

Whatever the meaning of their earlier encounter tonight, Sabrina knew she was long past playing games with Jules Danner. It was suddenly important to her to start over with a clean slate.

"I said that on impulse the other night," she said, her tone matching his. "It wasn't true. I've already told Ralph I have no intention of marrying him. I hardly expect that I'll see him again."

A small smile played at a corner of Jules's mouth. The frost had melted from his eyes. "Now, about Glenhaven—" he said.

"It's your house," Sabrina hastened to interrupt reasonably. "Never mind what I think about it. I'm irrelevant. If I don't like it, I don't have to look at it. There's nothing to stop me from turning my head away when I pass."

"If it were your home again, you would have to look

at it," Jules teased. "Though you could refuse to live there, I suppose." His voice goaded her for a reply.

"That's something I don't even have to consider," she said acidly, suddenly tired of her chosen role of darn good sport. "I leave you and your dear Rhonda to whatever esoteric pleasures you can find to enjoy in your wonderful new glass house."

From the other side of the hearth, Jules leaned forward to look at her incredulously for a moment before he burst into a hearty laugh.

"Sabrina! I believe you've been up to your old tricks again. You've been imagining things."

"Well?" she challenged hotly.

"You didn't really suppose there was something between the feisty decorator and me?" he asked. Then seeing her face, he laughed again. "You've got a lot to learn about me, dear Sabrina. I can't think of a better time to start than now."

He got up and crossed to her chair where he stood looking down at her from his full height, the craggy face suddenly serious and bathed in tenderness.

"You're such a creature of impulse, my beloved Princess! I can't take a chance on your jumping to false conclusions this time. Heaven help me if I do this any way but right," he said gravely, though she imagined she detected a hint of a twinkle in his eyes. Before her wondering eyes he went down on his knees in the best accepted tradition and poured words into her ears she had never, in her most wildly conceived fancies, hoped to hear from the lips of this man.

"Sabrina, dear, will you do me the honor of marrying me?"

Her heart thundering in her breast, Sabrina gazed at him numbly. She understood what he had said to her, but lately she found her ears had been getting her in a lot of trouble. The same prudent voice she had ignored a short time before told her that this time she must be sure.

In the sudden rapture of the moment, she was seized with a light-headedness that lent a dreamlike quality to the scene. Seated now on the deep pile carpet beside her chair, Jules reached out and eased her gently, unresisting, from her seat and into his arms.

"Sabrina, Sabrina," he murmured, his face against her hair. "I'm asking you to marry me, woman."

Out of the tumult of emotion within her, Sabrina at last found her voice and whispered, "Why?" In a tone of gentle amazement, Jules then said the words Sabrina realized she had waited all her life to hear.

"*Why?* Because I love you, of course," he said. "Because I've loved you ever since I was that boy back there, I suppose, although I didn't know it. When you came back into my life a few weeks ago, I knew why I'd been playing the field all these years. I'd been looking all my adult years for a particular kind of intelligent, beautiful, humorous, spunky woman; and lo and behold, I find it's the woman the little princess grew up to be. Tell me now, Sabrina. Will you live 'happily ever after' with me at Glenhaven?"

With these words, Jules washed the slate clean of all bitterness. They had arrived at the moment of the new beginning. Her heart sang with its music.

"Oh, Jules! I'd marry you if you asked me to live with you in a rabbit hutch," she said.

She was back in her dream again—only now it was

real. The arms that held her were flesh and blood. In the body that enfolded her she heard the hard, fierce beat of a heart. With her head cradled against his broad chest, Jules's strong, gentle fingers explored her face, passing lightly over her cheekbones, her forehead, along its perimeters from earlobe to chin.

No more were the dark eyes inscrutable but warm with love and a kind of wonder as if he had drawn back an opaque curtain to let her see the secrets within while he searched for meaning in hers. Her heart swelling with a new pervasive trust, Sabrina let her own loving secrets pour into her eyes for him to see.

As if to seal an unspoken bond that was to tie them together forever, Jules kissed her; softly at first but when their lips joined Sabrina knew—and was powerless to resist—a sudden inner acceleration. Turning in his arms, she hungrily gave her mouth to his. In a state of breathless suspension, she waited as his strong fingers moved along the line of silk that framed her throat and paused at the first closed button. In a moment, he had it unfastened to expose the full curves of her breast.

With a small, involuntary moan, Jules's head came down, and he buried his face in the soft, fragrant valley. Her heart thundered wildly next to his cheek. After a long moment, he raised his head and shook it lightly, as if to tear himself from a spell.

"Have mercy on me," he said, reluctance in every move as he let her go and sprang to his feet with a restless animal grace. He pulled her up beside him and gave her a gentle push. "I've just found out that my weakness is growing stronger than my strength," he said ruefully. "Until the vows are said, my lovely, do us both a favor and don't wear this—tantalizing garb."

Floating on air, Sabrina drifted obediently into her bedroom. Bemused and fumble-fingered in her impatience to get back to Jules, she changed into daytime dress. Thanks to her own clumsy haste, she had been several minutes away when she returned to find no Jules. Her start of alarm was stilled when she saw he had thrown a new log in the fire as if he expected to stay. She stepped to the door and from the stair landing saw a light shining into the downstairs hallway from the kitchen below.

There she found Jules down on one knee examining the golden retriever's paw. He looked up with a smile when she came in. Giving the dog an affectionate scratch under the collar, he got to his feet.

"I thought I'd better look in on our old friend," he said. "He seems to be doing well."

"He still has a couple of capsules to take. Maybe you'd help me to get one down him. It's a terrible job."

Jules took the capsule from her.

"Here, old man," he said to Hero. Catching the animal's head under one arm, he forced the jaws open, dropped in the medicine and held the mouth shut until a movement in the throat said the capsule had gone down. The deed was performed in one quick operation.

"Thanks," said Sabrina. "You should see me do it. He makes me wrestle him all over the kitchen."

Jules gave the big dog a conciliatory pat and turned back to Sabrina. "Come, Princess. We have many things to talk about," he said, drawing her into the circle of an arm and moving with her toward the hall.

On the lower landing, Sabrina looked back to where

Hero stood in the kitchen doorway, sad-eyed and alone. Filled to overflowing with her own happiness, Sabrina couldn't bear to shut him out.

"All right, chum," she called back to the retriever. "Just this one time, you can come too." As the dog came bounding joyfully to her, she glanced defensively at Jules to find him looking down at her, his eyes warm with loving amusement.

"It's not hard to see who will say all the no's to *our* children," he said, laughing fondly as he leaned down to kiss her.

Our children, Sabrina repeated silently to herself and wondered that a human heart could hold so much happiness.

Together they climbed the stairway arm in arm, with the red-gold dog lumbering up behind them, sore paw forgotten in the pleasure of acceptance. At the upper landing, Hero shot Sabrina a guilty look and, as if afraid he would be banished unless he established a beachhead, he pushed ahead of them and made for the fireplace where he curled up solidly on the hearth.

Sabrina and Jules came to a stop before him, and Jules enfolded her in his arms. "Mmm—*nice!*" he murmured and leaned to kiss her again. Their lips clung lightly, hungrily for a moment. Then he let her go and steered her to the love seat beside the hearth.

"We've wasted too much time already, Sabrina," he said seriously when she was curled up beside him in the curve of his arm. "I would like for us to be married right away, if you don't mind a short honeymoon. Right at the moment I'd rather we weren't away for more than a few days."

"Enough time for Niagara Falls?" she asked dreamily. "A friend of Aunt Hat's went there on her honeymoon when I was a little girl. I always thought it was the only way to go."

"Niagara Falls it is," Jules agreed with an amused laugh. "Later we'll take a second one—a cruise around the Greek islands, a boat down the Rhine—wherever you want to go. Right now I feel we are needed here to keep an eye on the work at Glenhaven."

The mention of Glenhaven fell like a dark shadow across Sabrina's rejoicing spirit. "Oh, yes—Glenhaven," she said quietly. "I'm sorry, Jules. I'm afraid I can't be of much help to you there."

"Of course you can," said Jules. "I'm counting on you to work as a close consultant to the architect."

Sabrina straightened and pulled herself out of the crook of his arm to look at him. She wanted to see if he was serious. She couldn't be sure.

"You've got to be joking. I wouldn't presume to discuss Glenhaven with—what's his name?—Mr. Fields? You're teasing me, Jules," she said in exasperation.

"Who said anything about Hadley Fields?" asked Jules, a glint of humor in his eyes. "Hadley's gone on to bigger and better things. Yesterday I went over to see the landmark people and hired a new man they recommended. He's already asked to consult with you and Aunt Harriet—wants to get the feel of the house as it was, he says. I think you'll find him all right."

Happiness swelled in Sabrina until it became a kind of joyous lump in her throat. For a moment she couldn't speak because of it. When she could, her voice sang in her ears.

"Oh, Jules! I can't believe it," she cried. "I thought you were completely in harmony with Mr. Fields. What made you change your mind?"

"I was until I saw what he had up his sleeve for Glenhaven. When I hired Fields, I told him to draw up something suitable for the house that would allow for more light and view on the river side. I've always thought the drawing room dark, and the narrow windows don't take full advantage of the view. I didn't spell it out. I just assumed he knew I meant to restore the place as it now stands, except for some minor modifications, not to redesign it into a late twentieth century showplace. Apparently the fellow thought I'd given him *carte blanche*. You saw it. What he came up with was bizarre."

Remembering, Sabrina said, "You hadn't seen the plans yet? You didn't know?"

"Not out there in front of the house that day. Things were moving fast at the plant, and I was busy. I knew Fields to be a first-rate architect, and I took it for granted he'd work out a suitable plan for the house without interference from me," he explained. "Then you came storming down the steps to take me apart that afternoon."

"I'm sorry," she murmured contritely.

"Don't be. It's true, I thought all you wanted was simply to heckle me, but just the same I decided I'd better take a look at those plans," he said. "Well, Hadley wasn't a bit interested in anything so mundane as restoring the old house, so we parted company."

Sabrina turned her head to look at him thoughtfully. No more did she have doubts about Jules's reasons, whatever they might be, but nonetheless she wondered. Her curiosity finally got the better of her.

"I've seen you since then, Jules. Why didn't you tell me? It could have saved some of the fuss over the restraining order."

Jules returned her query with a candid smile. "I tried. That's what Fields and Rhonda were to meet with me about that night you and Spurling took their places at my table. If you recall, I started to tell you then, but you shut me off cold. Then I began to wonder if the old house was *all* you cared about. I had to be sure that you could care for me without considering Glenhaven. Damned if I wanted to be in love with a woman who was capable of loving no more than a house."

Safe in his arms, knowing at last that Glenhaven would be safe, Sabrina sighed with a greater happiness than she'd ever dreamed it was possible to know. In one short evening she had been given so much. She suddenly felt that the time had come for her to give something in return. It would be hard, but she knew it had to be done.

"Ms. Bartlett is knowledgeable enough about antiques, I should think," she ventured sportingly at last. "Once she understands that monochromatic color schemes and modern furnishings are incompatible with an eighteenth century manor house, I'm sure—"

"Don't worry about Rhonda," Jules interrupted to assure her with a glint of mischief in his eyes. "I let her go, too. I said I had this great antique expert to do the decorating, once I persuaded her to be my wife."

Like a storm-tossed craft that has found safe harbor, Sabrina curled up in Jules's arms again and joined dreamily in wedding plans. So much had changed between them in so short a time, they soon lapsed into a pensive silence; wrapped in comfortable private thoughts, yet sharing the contentment of their new-found harmony of spirit.

Suddenly Hero, dozing on the hearth, lifted his head with a listening look. From the shop below there came a faraway, muffled chorus of the seven clocks as they chimed the hour of ten.

A smile crossed Jules's face. "Listen, Princess," he said softly. "They're playing our song."

But Sabrina, head pressed dreamily against Jules's chest, was hearing, over the rhythm of his swiftly beating heart, the wild, sweet sound of those other bells she had been listening for more than half her life.

Silhouette ❤ *Romance*

15-Day Free Trial Offer
6 Silhouette Romances

6 Silhouette Romances, free for 15 days! We'll send you 6 new Silhouette Romances to keep for 15 days, absolutely free! If you decide not to keep them, send them back to us. You pay nothing.

Free Home Delivery. But if you enjoy them as much as we think you will, keep them by paying the invoice enclosed with your free trial shipment. We'll pay all shipping and handling charges. You get the convenience of Home Delivery and we pay the postage and handling charge each month.

Don't miss a copy. The Silhouette Book Club is the way to make sure you'll be able to receive every new romance we publish before they're sold out. There is no minimum number of books to buy and you can cancel at any time.

Silhouette Romance

IT'S YOUR OWN SPECIAL TIME

Contemporary romances for today's women.
Each month, six very special love stories will be yours
from SILHOUETTE. Look for them wherever books are sold
or order now from the coupon below.

$1.50 each

Hampson	☐ 1 ☐ 4 ☐ 16 ☐ 27 ☐ 28 ☐ 40 ☐ 52 ☐ 64 ☐ 94	Browning	☐ 12 ☐ 38 ☐ 53 ☐ 73 ☐ 93
Stanford	☐ 6 ☐ 25 ☐ 35 ☐ 46 ☐ 58 ☐ 88	Michaels	☐ 15 ☐ 32 ☐ 61 ☐ 87
		John	☐ 17 ☐ 34 ☐ 57 ☐ 85
Hastings	☐ 13 ☐ 26 ☐ 44 ☐ 67	Beckman	☐ 8 ☐ 37 ☐ 54 ☐ 72 ☐ 96
Vitek	☐ 33 ☐ 47 ☐ 66 ☐ 84		

$1.50 each

☐ 5 Goforth	☐ 29 Wildman	☐ 56 Trent	☐ 79 Halldorson
☐ 7 Lewis	☐ 30 Dixon	☐ 59 Vernon	☐ 80 Stephens
☐ 9 Wilson	☐ 31 Halldorson	☐ 60 Hill	☐ 81 Roberts
☐ 10 Caine	☐ 36 McKay	☐ 62 Hallston	☐ 82 Dailey
☐ 11 Vernon	☐ 39 Sinclair	☐ 63 Brent	☐ 83 Halston
☐ 14 Oliver	☐ 41 Owen	☐ 69 St. George	☐ 86 Adams
☐ 19 Thornton	☐ 42 Powers	☐ 70 Afton Bonds	☐ 89 James
☐ 20 Fulford	☐ 43 Robb	☐ 71 Ripy	☐ 90 Major
☐ 21 Richards	☐ 45 Carroll	☐ 74 Trent	☐ 92 McKay
☐ 22 Stephens	☐ 48 Wildman	☐ 75 Carroll	☐ 95 Wisdom
☐ 23 Edwards	☐ 49 Wisdom	☐ 76 Hardy	☐ 97 Clay
☐ 24 Healy	☐ 50 Scott	☐ 77 Cork	☐ 98 St. George
	☐ 55 Ladame	☐ 78 Oliver	☐ 99 Camp

$1.75 each

☐ 100 Stanford	☐ 105 Eden	☐ 110 Trent	☐ 115 John
☐ 101 Hardy	☐ 106 Dailey	☐ 111 South	☐ 116 Lindley
☐ 102 Hastings	☐ 107 Bright	☐ 112 Stanford	☐ 117 Scott
☐ 103 Cork	☐ 108 Hampson	☐ 113 Browning	☐ 118 Dailey
☐ 104 Vitek	☐ 109 Vernon	☐ 114 Michaels	☐ 119 Hampson